CHR☉NAL
ENGINE

by GREG LEITICH SMITH

with illustrations by BLAKE HENRY

Clarion Books >< Houghton Mifflin Harcourt >< Boston   New York
2012

BOCA RATON PUBLIC LIBRARY
BOCA RATON, FLORIDA

Clarion Books

215 Park Avenue South, New York, New York 10003

Copyright © 2012 by Greg H. Leitich

Illustrations copyright © 2012 by Blake Henry

All rights reserved. For information about permission to reproduce selections from this book,
write to Permissions, Houghton Mifflin Harcourt Publishing Company,
215 Park Avenue South, New York, New York 10003.

Clarion Books is an imprint of Houghton Mifflin Harcourt Publishing Company.

www.hmhbooks.com

The text was set in Mundo Sans.

Library of Congress Cataloging-in-Publication Data

Smith, Greg Leitich.

Chronal Engine / by Greg Leitich Smith ; illustrated by Blake Henry.

p. cm.

Summary: Eighth-grader Max, his older brother Kyle, and new friend Petra travel in time to the Cretaceous period
to rescue Kyle's twin, Emma, who was kidnapped from their grandfather's Texas ranch.

Includes author's notes about the facts behind the story,

Includes bibliographical references.

ISBN 978-0-547-60849-5

[1. Time travel—Fiction. 2. Dinosaurs—Fiction. 3. Brothers and sisters—Fiction. 4. Twins—Fiction. 5. Kidnapping—Fiction.
6. Paleontology—Fiction. 7. Grandfathers—Fiction. 8. Texas—Fiction. 9. Science fiction.] I. Henry, Blake, ill. II. Title.

PZ7.S6488Chr 2012

[Fic]—dc23

2011027483

Manufactured in the United States of America

DOC 10 9 8 7 6 5 4 3 2 1

4500342964

< To Ginger >

TODAY

"JUST HOW MUCH OF A CREEPY OLD HERMIT MAN IS HE, AGAIN?"
my sister, Emma, asked as Mom drove us up the hill to my grandfather's ranch house.

It wasn't a ranch-*style* house, but a house that sat on a five-
thousand-acre ranch with cattle and everything.

The building itself was a three-story 1890s Texas Victorian
mansion built into the side of a hill. It had a cupola, a raised wraparound porch with outside ceiling fans, and burgundy and purple
trim around the windows and eaves.

"Because this doesn't look that bad," Emma went on, glancing
at us in the back seat. "What do you think, guys?"

My brother, Kyle—Emma's twin—just grunted.

"Max?" Mom prompted.

"It's, um, freshly painted," I said, which, okay, wasn't much better than Kyle's grunt, but still.

"It's exactly as I remember it," Mom said as she brought the
Tahoe to a halt.

Kyle grunted again. It had been two weeks, and he still hadn't
forgiven Mom for springing the news on us that she'd been of-

fered a position (and a fast-track grant and visa) to go to some remote corner of Mongolia on a dig for feathered dinosaurs that were supposed to be even more spectacular than the ones from Liaoning Province, China. It was very last minute, but the paleontological institute over there had asked for Mom—Dr. Ernestine Pierson-Takahashi—"by name," she'd said. It was apparently an enormous compliment, a terrific opportunity, and one of those things you couldn't say no to.

With our dad having died five years ago in Afghanistan and my uncle (Mom's brother) working in London, that left my grandfather as the only one who could realistically have taken us in. And so, in an act of extreme desperation, Mom had asked her father if he'd do it, and, to her enormous surprise, he'd said yes.

The thing was, despite the fact that the ranch was only thirty minutes from where we lived in west Austin, Mom had seen Grandpa only once in nearly fifteen years, and the three of us had met him only on that same occasion, at Dad's funeral.

Supposedly, Grandpa just decided one day that he'd had enough of people and family, and people like family, and since then had left the ranch just that one time. The only humans he talked to were his ranch foreman and the lady who cooked and cleaned for him.

From what I understood, this sort of thing wasn't completely unusual in our family: the guy who'd built the house—my grandfather's grandfather—was nicknamed "Mad Jack" Pierson because he'd spent most of his fortune to build what he'd claimed was a time machine, which he called the "Chronal Engine."

Not surprisingly, he'd died a recluse.

So Kyle, Emma, and I weren't exactly thrilled to be trapped all summer in the middle of nowhere on a ranch with a complete stranger. Probably I was most looking forward to it, because I was the only one of the three of us who'd picked up what Mom called the family "dinosaur gene." She had it, she'd said, from having grown up here. (This isn't how genetics works, of course, but sometimes my mother is ironic.)

Anyway, the ranch was home to the famous Loblolly Dinosaur Tracks, sets of fossilized Late Cretaceous footprints attributed to *Tyrannosaurus rex*, among others, in one of the Colorado River tributary creeks that ran on the ranch.

I'd never seen the tracks, of course, and neither had an entire generation of paleontologists—my grandfather had caused something of an uproar when he'd stopped allowing them onto the ranch, too. My mother was still hearing about this from unhappy colleagues and the occasional frustrated PhD candidate.

As we got out of the car in front of the house, though, it was hard not to be impressed. The mansion was situated on a hill above the Colorado River and had an incredible view. We could see for miles in every direction: the river snaking its way, eventually, to the Gulf; the pines and live oaks; the hills of McKinney Roughs rising in the distance; and the gathering rain clouds.

"Little Buddy Creek is down that way." Mom gestured vaguely toward the woods off to the left, where the dinosaur tracks were.

As Kyle and I pulled our suitcases out of the back of the Tahoe, the front door of the house opened and a seventy-ish man, leaning heavily on a black lacquered cane, strode across the porch to stand at the top of the steps. He was tall—taller than I'd expected—had bushy white hair, and was wearing boots, jeans, and a red, long-sleeved Western shirt.

He paused, peering down the flight of stairs.

"Hold on a second, kids," Mom said, then ran up to greet him. She and her father hugged for a long moment.

After they talked for a while, she gestured for us to come up.

Up close, I thought our grandfather looked more like the twins than me. He had Emma's dark eyes and good posture, but Kyle's straight nose and unruly hair.

He gave each of us a long, appraising look.

"High school?" he asked the twins.

"Freshman year," Emma answered. "In the fall."

"You're the one who plays football?" he asked Kyle.

My brother nodded. "Hoping to make varsity this year."

It was one of the reasons Kyle was so angry about having to come here. He and his friend Jordan had had great plans for "off-season conditioning" this summer, which, so far as I could tell, involved a lot of running and the repetitive lifting of metal plates.

Mom had told him that Uncle Nate's old weight set was probably gathering dust in the basement here, but Kyle was still mad.

Personally, I didn't think the two of them had much of a chance at varsity, anyway, but I wasn't going to say that aloud.

"And you're the flutist?" Grandpa asked Emma.

"And the swimmer and the lifeguard trainee and the math geek and the hospice volunteer and the sister," Emma said with a bright smile that had kind of an edge to it. "I'm a lot of things."

Everything she'd said was true, and she did them all well, which was occasionally irritating, especially when people asked me what I did.

When they bothered to, anyway.

"Dinosaurs?" they'd repeat, and give me kind of a funny look.

"And you're Max?" Grandpa said to me.

I nodded.

He stared at me for a moment. "Eighth grade?"

I nodded again. "In the fall."

He just squinted at me, but had no more questions. "Y'all can have the run of the place," he said finally, "so long as y'all don't stampede the cattle and don't bother me none, either."

"See? It's not so bad," said Emma, who is almost always optimistic but not annoying about it.

After Mom had left (with that pinched look and the line

between her eyebrows), the three of us had been introduced to Mrs. Castillo, Grandpa's assistant/nurse/cook.

Then we moved our things into our respective rooms on the second floor. Kyle and I were in rooms with a connecting door, and Emma was across the hall.

Once I'd dumped my clothes into the dresser drawers and plugged my laptop in to charge, I headed downstairs to the parlor to look around. (I knew it would take Emma and Kyle a lot longer to unpack because they believed in hanging up and folding their clothes.)

Like all the rooms in the house, the parlor was centered around a fireplace. This one was built of some green tile and was topped with a black granite mantel. A seating area—including a cowhide sofa and leather pillows, a pair of wing chairs, and a coffee table—faced the fireplace. To the side stood a five-shelf leaded-glass barrister's bookcase filled with books about the Loblolly Tracks.

When it began to rain, I flicked on a reading lamp, pulled one of the books off the shelf, and stretched out on the sofa to read, careful of the volume's yellowing pages. The book had been published in the early 1940s, about fifteen years after the discovery of the tracks themselves, so its discussion of dinosaurs was mostly out-of-date. *Tyrannosaurus rex* did *not* drag its tail, and the sauropods probably *weren't* swimming.

I was deep in the details of how James R. Wainwright, a prospector for Humboldt Oil, had stumbled upon the footprints, when I felt hands drumming my head.

"Kyle," I said, turning around, to see him and Emma. "You're such a—"

He snatched the book from my hands.

"Hey!" I tried to grab it back, but not too hard, because I didn't want to tear the pages.

"Don't be such a big giant dork," Kyle said, tossing the book onto the wing chair next to him. "Let's go explore!"

"I was reading, you troglodyte." I did wonder about Kyle's sudden enthusiasm for the place. Maybe Emma had talked to him. Or maybe he was just bored. "It's raining, or, believe me, I'd've already been out to see the tracks myself by now."

We were interrupted by the sound of someone clearing his throat. Without a word, Grandpa strode from the arched entryway, around the front of the coffee table, to stand by the wing chair. He picked up the book, leafed through it once. "Boy your age should be outside in the summertime."

I began, "But—"

"Out! All of you, out!" he said, waving the volume in the air.

Emma opened the front door and led the way onto the porch. As I looked back, Grandpa made another shooing motion.

I closed the door behind us and stepped across the porch to look at the view.

Emma sat cross-legged on a wicker patio chair. "What was that all about?"

"Boy your age shouldn't be sitting around reading," Kyle said, in a passable imitation of our grandfather. He paused. "What was the book?"

"Why?" I asked, suspicious and still annoyed with him. I sat up on the porch railing and grabbed the column to balance myself.

"He took it with him," Kyle noted, as he eased himself into a wooden rocking chair. "He didn't put it back on the shelf."

I didn't know why Grandpa would've wanted it. "It was just about the history of the place."

After a while the rain stopped, and as we sat watching a pair of hawks circle overhead, a girl about our age came marching up the driveway.

She caught my attention for a couple reasons.

First, she was really attractive. She was a little shorter than me and lightly freckled. Her dark hair had been pulled back in a ponytail.

Second, she was carrying a recurve hunting bow in one hand and a game bag over her shoulder. She clomped up the steps in her hiking boots and dropped the bag onto the porch.

"Y'all like rabbit?" she asked, lifting an eyebrow.

"Tastes like chicken," Emma replied, although not from any personal experience that I knew of.

"Good," the girl answered, "then you can help me dress 'em."

"What about us?" Kyle asked. He put on his most winning
smile, so I could tell he thought she was cute too.

"What about us?" Kyle asked. He put on his most winning smile, so I could tell he thought she was cute too.

She gave him a long look and me a shorter one. "Y'all can catch your own."

At Emma's laugh, the girl picked up the game bag and led my sister around the wraparound porch to the back.

Turning the corner, she looked over her shoulder. "My name's Petra. My mother works here. Pleased to meet you."

She didn't wait for us to introduce ourselves.

When I figured the two were out of earshot, I told Kyle, "I don't think you're her type."

He grinned. "Maybe it won't be so bad here, after all."

Chapter

II

LEGACY

DESPITE ITS WILD BEGINNING, THE *HASENPFEFFER* FOR DINNER that night was excellently prepared by Mrs. Castillo according to an old family recipe and was served on white china with sterling silverware in the formal dining room.

My grandfather, framed by the leaded-glass windows behind him, sat at the head of the heavy antique table, and, for the occasion, Mrs. Castillo sat opposite him. Kyle and I were on one side. Emma and Petra, who had become fast friends over skinning and disemboweling our main course, were across from us.

The table could've easily seated twelve. An enormous carved oak fireplace covered the wall behind Kyle and me. To Petra's and Emma's backs stood a built-in buffet and china cabinet with a pass-through to a butler's pantry beyond.

Hanging from the twelve-foot ceiling above was a crystal chandelier, which, according to my grandfather, had made the trip from Ireland at the turn of the century unscathed but now, for some reason he'd been unclear about, had at least a half-dozen cracked crystals.

Grandpa spent most of the meal concentrating on his "masti-

< 11 >

cation," which required effort since he would chew each mouthful a particular number of times depending on whether it was animal or vegetable. It was for his health, he'd said, and had named various portions of his gastrointestinal tract this supposedly helped.

It did make eating stew sort of a challenge, which was why I think Mrs. Castillo made it.

It turned out that she and Mom had been friends back in high school and had kept in touch, at least through Christmas cards.

The rest of us were having kind of a fun time, discussing whether Mom would ever actually drink yak's milk and whether the stuff was really pink, when my grandfather took a sip of wine and put down his napkin. "It is time."

The room went silent, except for the ticking of the mantel clock.

"It is time," Grandpa began again, and looked at Emma, Kyle, and me in turn, "for you to see the family legacy. Downstairs. In the workshop. Petra, this concerns you as well."

"You don't want dessert?" Mrs. Castillo asked, setting her napkin beside her plate and looking vaguely alarmed. "The pecan pie will be ready in a moment."

Grandpa stood. "Perhaps the children would like some when we're done. As for me . . ." He hesitated. "Thank you, no. In fifteen minutes the ambulance will be here to take me to the hospital after my massive heart attack."

I stared. "What did you just say?"

Grandpa raised his hand. "We don't have much time."

Mrs. Castillo nodded. "Go on, then."

Neither Mrs. Castillo nor Grandpa seemed to be reacting like anything unusual was happening. But when I glanced across the table, Emma shrugged and gave me what I interpreted as a "he's probably not dangerous and he is our grandfather" look, so I just swallowed my qualms, put down my fork, and decided to go with it, too.

At least for the moment.

Grandpa led us to the basement stairs, flicking on the lights as he opened the door. "Max," he said, and put a hand on my shoulder, "promise me that tomorrow morning at eight, before it gets too hot, you and the others will go out to the fossil track way."

By now I was starting to kind of freak out. "Me? Why? I was planning to—"

"Promise!" He stepped closer. "Be there at eight!"

"All right," I said, glancing back at Kyle and Emma, who both nodded. "I will. We will." Like I'd tried to tell him, I'd been planning to go, anyway, but why was he so insistent? He hadn't seemed at all interested in what I did earlier today.

We followed Grandpa down the curving staircase. Crystal sconces lit the way, although we couldn't see what lay beyond the curve.

At the bottom, Grandpa handed me an envelope. It felt heavy, expensive. "Open this later."

He waited until I told him I would, and I slipped the envelope into a pocket of my cargo shorts. Then he gestured with his cane, presenting the room.

The "workshop," he'd called it, but it looked more like a library. Oak paneling and built-in bookcases lined the walls. A red and gold rug covered the concrete floor. A wooden desk and a pair of workbenches were on the far side, under the front windows, next to the French doors. There weren't any computers, but a bulky microfiche reader sat on one of the worktables.

A three-foot-long lobe-finned fish—a coelacanth—was mounted on a pedestal in one of the bookcases. Resting on another shelf was a chicken-sized skeleton of what looked like a *Compsognathus*, an early theropod dinosaur from the Triassic. I assumed it was a cast.

"That's it?" Emma asked, drawing my attention away from the displays.

Grandpa pulled back a velvet curtain to reveal the machine that occupied a good quarter of the room.

"My grandfather's greatest achievement," he said. "Perhaps the greatest achievement in the history of mankind." His face grew sad. "Also, his greatest tragedy."

The Chronal Engine. It was about the size of a compact pickup truck. Resembling the 1930s console radio in the upstairs parlor, it had a central cabinet that looked like a coppery-metallic curved rectangle with two smaller sections on either side.

Multiple brass levers and switches, a quartet of glass dials, and a number of old-time light bulbs with visible, glowing filaments were set into its main body. A round CRT screen, now dark, was centered above the dials. On top sat a larger light, about the size of a milk jug, inside a wire cage.

"It has its own generator," Grandpa said, as we gathered around.

Off to the side of the Engine stood a locked glass case, one shelf holding a brass and glass sphere about the size of a baseball.

"This," Grandpa announced, "is a Recall Device. The time traveler uses it to set temporal-spatial coordinates and activates it to return to the present."

"So it's a remote control," I put in.

"Yes, but not quite," Grandpa said. He sighed. "This is the last one."

I looked closer through the glass door of the case. The Device was intricately inscribed with gradations and numerals, like a precision instrument—as fine as the detailing on the antique slide rule my mom kept on her desk. Stripes along the side indicated where the pieces could move relative to one another.

The whole thing was creeping me out. "What do we do?" I whispered to my brother.

"Keep humoring him," Kyle answered.

Before I could respond, I heard a noise outside. It took me a moment to figure out what it was. "Is that a helicopter?"

"Ah." With a slight smile, Grandpa turned to Petra. "Your mother

Off to the side of the Engine stood a locked glass case, one shelf holding a brass and glass sphere, about the size of a baseball.

is an excellent woman." Then he clutched at his chest and collapsed.

Kyle leaped forward, catching him before his head hit the side of the machine, while Petra yelled, "Mom!"

Grandpa tried to raise a hand and whispered something to Kyle. My brother nodded, frowning, as he helped Grandpa lie back on the floor.

At the same time, I heard Mrs. Castillo's footsteps clatter down the stairs.

"Med Flight is here!" She dashed across the room and opened the French doors from the basement to the lawn where the helicopter was landing. Then she ran out and waved. "Over here!"

Moments later the paramedics arrived with a gurney and defibrillator.

"Kids, go upstairs," Mrs. Castillo said. "There's pecan pie and Blue Bell ice cream on the table. I'll go with Mr. Pierson and call you when we get to the hospital."

"But—" Kyle began.

"Do it!" Mrs. Castillo said.

Petra led the way, with Emma following closely behind.

At the bottom of the stairs, I grabbed Kyle by the arm. "What did he say to you?"

Kyle shook his head, forehead wrinkled. "He said, 'Take the bug.' Do you know what he was talking about?"

"No."

Other than the fish and the *Compsognathus,* there was a bunch of natural history museum-type samples lying around—a human skull, a bird skeleton—but no bugs.

"What's in the envelope he gave you?" Kyle asked.

"I don't know," I replied. "Let's check it out upstairs."

As we hurried up, my mind was racing. No matter how calm he and Mrs. Castillo had seemed, I couldn't help worrying about Grandpa, even if we barely knew him. How had he predicted his own heart attack? Was he psychic? Or did he receive a message from the future?

If so, that meant the Chronal Engine *worked.*

Upstairs we found a plate with a slice of pecan pie at each of our place settings. A tub of ice cream sat in a bowl filled with ice at the center of the table.

"That was really, really strange," Emma said, leaning over the back of her chair. "How did the helicopter get here so quickly?"

"Not just quickly," I told her. "It was here *before* he had the heart attack. He mentioned it at dinner. He knew ahead of time that something was going to happen."

"How?" Emma asked.

"It's obvious." I paused. "The Chronal Engine works."

"The time machine?" Kyle said. "What, did Santa Claus pull the switch?"

"Yeah, okay," I said. "But you all heard it. Grandpa said it would be in fifteen minutes, and it was."

"There has to be a better explanation than a time machine," Kyle replied.

Emma nodded. "Maybe he just felt the heart attack coming on."

"Before we sat down to dinner?" I asked. "You think that's possible?"

Kyle shrugged. "Has to be."

I snorted.

Annoyed that they were doing the "twin support in all things" thing, I sat at my place and scooped some ice cream—Mexican vanilla—onto my plate.

"How can you eat?" Emma asked as I took a mouthful of ice cream and pie.

"Good pie," I said, and opened the envelope.

"What is it?" Kyle asked.

"A map." I spread it out on the table.

It was a printed map of the creek with the dinosaur footprints, from back in the days when the ranch was open to tourists and paleontologists. It looked a little like one of the maps in the book Grandpa had taken, but there was something different.

Kyle came around to peer over my shoulder. "And *X* marks the spot."

A black *X* was scrawled on the map near the creek, a little re-moved from the main body of track beds.

I showed Petra the paper. "What's there?"

"Nothing I can think of." She bit her lip. "It's sort of overgrown with brush and . . . I think it's just an area that's never been cleared out."

At a flash of lightning, Emma got up and looked out the window. Big droplets of rain splattered against the panes. "Tomorrow morning?"

I nodded, still staring at the map. What could be marked there? Maybe Grandpa had discovered some kind of new dinosaur. But why would he insist on our going to the site the day after he'd had a heart attack that he'd known about in advance?

After an hour or so of talking in circles, we cleaned up the dining room and kitchen and then got a phone call from Mrs. Castillo. Grandpa was still in critical condition, and she'd call again when there was more news.

I wondered how much Grandpa had known. Did he know he was going to come out of it all right? Or did he know he was going to die? If so, why hadn't he done anything to prevent the attack?

< 20 >

FOOTPRINTS IN THE STONE

MRS. CASTILLO CALLED AGAIN AT ELEVEN THIRTY THAT NIGHT TO tell us that the doctors were optimistic, but Grandpa was still "touch and go."

The rain still hadn't slackened off by midnight.

At twelve thirty Petra grabbed an umbrella and headed down the hill to the cottage she and her mother lived in, while Emma, Kyle, and I went up to bed.

I lay awake for a while thinking about Grandpa and the Chronal Engine, and eventually decided to go down to the workshop and check things out.

On my way, I remembered the history book Grandpa had taken, so I took a detour to his room. The door was locked, though, so I went on down to the parlor.

The book hadn't been reshelved.

I continued to the basement. The lights of the Chronal Engine glowed softly, and the large bulb in the cage on top flickered every now and then. The machine felt warm to the touch.

When I put my ear to it, I could hear a low hum, though it was hard to make out over the air conditioner.

I didn't really know what I was looking for. Something, maybe, about how the Chronal Engine worked or even just a clue on why Mad Jack had built the thing in the first place.

I didn't know where to start, but I lucked out when I pulled open the top filing cabinet drawer closest to the desk. It contained what looked like lab books.

I grabbed two volumes and set them on the desk, clicked on the green banker's reading light, and began to leaf through the first. The pages were covered with crabbed, handwritten scribblings and equations. Other pages had scraps of paper, notes, and correspondence pasted in. Still more pages had rough diagrams of machine parts and specifications. Both the math and the accompanying text were baffling.

Glued to the first page was a sheet of stationery with the letterhead of the Hotel Adolphus in Dallas. It read:

> *Dr. Einstein's relativity implies space-time pinholes,*
> *requiring infinite gravity.*
>
> *But this came to me during the game today:*
> *quantum tunneling of pseudogravity particles and*
> *modulation of resulting chronal wave with field-*
> *resonant material should make instantaneous*
> *temporal inversion of massive objects possible.*

Also on the sheet was a diagram of a sphere with a group of lines radiating from one point on its surface, through its interior, to other points on its surface.

I sat back. This must've been when Mad Jack had first conceived of the Chronal Engine. His greatest achievement, Grandpa had said. And I didn't understand a word of it.

As I read on, it became clear that Professor Pierson's experiments had been somewhat controversial. His paper had been rejected for publication six times, and his department head had called him a "dangerous quack." An appeal to Albert Einstein by telegram went unanswered.

So Pierson built the Chronal Engine in secrecy at a lab at the University of Texas. But his lab assistant and some of the other scientists eventually went to the engineering dean to try to shut him down.

Pierson became convinced that his colleagues were trying to steal his work, and he tried to test the Engine before they could turn it off or take it away and destroy it or something. Unfortunately, in the process, he accidentally overloaded the power grid and blacked out the whole town.

When the dean finally closed down the project, Pierson carted the Engine here to the ranch and, like Thomas Edison, built his own power station.

When I finished reading the first book, I moved on to the second.

"What language is this?" I muttered.

"What language is *what?*" Emma replied from the stairwell, startling me. She came into the light at the bottom of the stairs, carrying a paper bag in one hand and a water pistol in the other, which she proceeded to shoot me with.

It was classic Emma, but I wasn't in the mood for it.

"What are you doing?" I asked, holding up my hand to deflect the water from my face and protect the lab book.

"Found this in Mom's old room," she said, gesturing with the water pistol. "What language is what?"

She sat and put the pistol down on the desk.

"This." I slid the book toward her. "I think it's Japanese. When did he learn Japanese?"

"Who?"

"Mad—" I began, then corrected myself. "Great-Great-Grandpa Pierson. This is his lab book. One of his lab books." I turned the page and saw something even more surprising. Then I turned another. And another. And two more. "This is incredible."

"What?"

I got up and opened the file cabinet to check out the remaining two books. They were the same. "This is incredible!"

"You already said that," Emma replied.

I set the books on the table and showed Emma the pages. "This page is Japanese, this is German, this is Russian, this is French, and

I don't know what these next two are. And then back to Japanese and so on. All the books are like that."

I was silent a moment, awed by the effort it would've taken.

"Looks like Gramps really, really didn't want anyone else to read his notebooks," Emma said.

"Yeah." I leaned back in the chair. "You don't think Petra's ever noticed anything weird out here before, do you?"

Emma leafed through one of the notebooks. "She did say that tonight had been the first time she'd ever been down in the basement. You still think the Chronal Engine works?"

I shrugged. "How else could Grandpa have known when his heart attack was going to occur, down to the minute?"

"Maybe he's psychic."

I rolled my eyes. "Yeah, right."

She laughed.

While she was distracted, I grabbed the water pistol and pointed it at her.

"You don't want to do that, Baby Brother," Emma said.

I hated when she called me that, although not as much as when Kyle did. (She called him Big Brother because he was older by about a minute and a half.)

"Why?" I asked. "Only you get to—"

"Because I have this." She reached down into the bag and pulled out a Super Soaker water cannon.

I froze. "Okay, you really don't want to do that in here. Old papers, books, strange machinery . . ."

"Maybe not." She looked thoughtful. "This isn't for you, anyway."

I raised an eyebrow, but lowered the pistol.

"I think Big Brother needs a change of attitude, don't you?" Emma asked. "He's been kind of a jerk lately. He could use . . . well, a wake-up call."

As she brandished the soaker, I broke into a grin. Kyle had been a pain these past few weeks. Sometimes, though, Emma could be dangerously whimsical. "He'll kill me."

She waved a hand. "Oh, he'll think about it, but would never actually go through with anything terminal."

"Oh, thanks."

"Besides," Emma went on, "we have this." She reached into the bag again and pulled out a compact video camera.

"Isn't that Mom's?" I asked.

"Yeah, but she got a new one for the Mongolia trip." Emma shrugged. "I shoot, you record, and if he gets any ideas, just threaten to upload the video."

I hesitated.

"You think he's going to want his future varsity teammates seeing him in a web video waking up and screaming like a girl?" She shook the soaker, so I could hear the clunking of . . .

"*Ice* cubes?" I exclaimed.

She nodded solemnly.

"Remind me never to get you mad at me . . ."

I opened the connecting door from my room and turned on the camera and the lights.

Kyle was snoring softly, sleeping on his side, one arm over the covers.

Emma entered through the main door, let out a piercing yell, and unleashed the full power of the Super Soaker water cannon.

The result was spectacular, although it didn't go exactly according to plan.

Instead of simply shocking Kyle awake with the ice water, a good part of it apparently went up his nose.

He didn't scream.

Instead, he sat up bolt upright, eyes bugging out, and coughing and gurgling like he was trying to get rid of a lung.

Emma stopped firing as soon as he sat up, but he was still completely drenched, hair plastered to his head, water dripping down his face.

"What the . . . what are you doing?" He brushed his hair out of his eyes. "Emma! Max!" Then he coughed again and snorted, scowling.

I lowered the camera uncertainly while Emma walked over and sat down in the cowhide wing chair. Crossing her legs, she laid the water cannon across her lap and began toying with the little gold cross she wore around her neck.

"Max," she said, "I think Big Bro and I are going to have a talk."

I left, for once not annoyed at being dismissed like a little kid by the two of them.

"Good night," I said, and left, aware of Kyle's gaze following my every step until I closed the connecting door.

Then I heard arguing, but couldn't make out what was being said.

Before I went to bed, I downloaded the video to my laptop.

The next morning I was awake first and got into the bathroom ahead of Kyle. As I came out, I ran into him leaving his room.

"You," he said, "are so dead."

"YouTube," I replied.

His expression didn't change.

Still, down at breakfast, he seemed more relaxed, more like himself than he'd been in a while, so Emma's plan seemed to have worked. But when I pulled her aside to ask what she'd said to him, she wouldn't tell me.

Petra arrived a few minutes after that, and at seven thirty we headed out to the track site. Petra led the way, with Emma beside her and carrying the video camera, while Kyle and I followed in their muddy footsteps.

The ground and undergrowth were still soaked from the rain,

so even though there was a well-defined path through the woods from the house to Little Buddy Creek, we were still pretty wet by the time we got there, our shoes caked in mud.

We passed the tree line to emerge on a slight crest overlooking the creek. A light mist lay over the water, saturating the air. Above the burble of the water, we could hear the calls of songbirds and the chirping of insects.

Below us, preserved for millions of years in the rock, three-toed *Tyrannosaurus rex* tracks paralleled the creek for about a hundred yards before crossing into it. Downstream a little were other tracks, thought to be from a herd of sauropod-type dino-saurs, maybe *Alamosaurus*. The water itself was too muddy from the rain to make out the ones in the creek bed itself, though I'd seen pictures in books.

I wanted to go down and take a closer look, but first I grabbed the map from my pocket and tried to orient myself.

Emma pulled the camera out of its case and panned up and down the creek.

"Over there, right?" I asked, and pointed to an area where vines and undergrowth formed a dense thicket.

"Yeah," Kyle said, after glancing at the map. He strode over to push through the scrubby growth.

I followed right behind him, Petra in back of me, and Emma bringing up the rear with the camera.

After a bit of a struggle, we were through and emerged above a small, two-foot-wide rocky stream, a tributary of the creek itself.

"This is it?" Kyle asked, turning in a circle.

Over the years, a trickle had carved its way through the rock, although now the water level looked higher than normal, thanks to the rain last night.

I stepped down into the streambed, onto a rock that lay halfway between the banks. From there I spotted three-toed bipedal theropod dinosaur footprints, a little longer than my own foot.

But there were also footprints of another biped that didn't belong there.

"Oh, wow," I said.

"So?" Kyle stepped into the water beside me. "They're footprints. So what?"

"They're *fossilized* footprints," I said, careful of my balance on the rock. "Of *humans* in hiking shoes. You can see the tread. In the same strata as the dinosaur tracks. Look, you can see some kind of theropod tracks just behind them . . . " I swallowed. "Which means, we know that someone, some *human*, was there in the time of the dinosaurs."

By now Emma had splashed across the stream, her camera pointed at the footprints. She put her right foot down next to a left shoe track, her boot lining up alongside. And then she stepped into it with her left boot.

It was a perfect fit.

"Get away from her!" Kyle shouted.

"Emma," Petra said, her voice hushed, "what does your tread look like?"

My sister lifted up her foot so we could see.

"It's the same!" Kyle exclaimed.

I was just about to say, "I told you the Chronal Engine works," when there was a flash of light on the creek bank and a man appeared from nowhere next to Emma.

He shoved Petra toward the rocks in the stream. She stumbled, but Kyle caught her before she fell.

The man was wearing a tweed jacket with a vest and a straw hat that looked like something he'd stolen from a barbershop quartet. Or from another time.

He was holding a Recall Device in one hand and a revolver in the other.

Before any of us could react, he had his arm around Emma's neck from behind.

"Get away from her!" Kyle shouted.

But the man gestured with the hand that held the Recall Device.

"Emma!" I shouted, and launched myself toward her. "Kyle! Don't let him—"

It was too late.

There was another flash of light and a booming sound, and then both my sister and the man were gone.

ONCE UPON A TIME . . .

"WHERE'D SHE GO?" KYLE TURNED TOWARD ME, HIS FACE PALE.
"Who was that? Was that Mad Jack Pierson?"

"No," I said. "I don't think so." At least it didn't look like the photos of him in the workshop. This guy was shorter and stockier, with darker hair.

"I don't care who he is," Petra said. "I ever see him again, I'm going to gut him like a fish."

Kyle gripped my shoulders. "What is going on? Where's Emma?"

"I don't know." I swallowed. "She might be in the Cretaceous. Because of the footprints." Which was completely terrifying. There was a reason the largest mammals back then were the size of house cats. And it wasn't just carnivores like *Tyrannosaurus rex* or *Utahraptor*—it was the herds of giant herbivores, too, like *Triceratops* and the hadrosaurs that could trample any primate flat.

But we knew Emma had been okay when she got there.

At least she'd been okay enough to leave footprints.

I just hoped she'd stayed that way.

"Wait. You're saying that guy, whoever he was, kidnapped her and took her back to the time of the dinosaurs?" Kyle stepped back. He glanced at the tracks and then back at me. "Why?"

"I don't know," I said. "Look, Grandpa sent us here for a reason at this exact time . . . to see those footprints. Maybe he knows something about whoever took Emma."

"What do you know about Grandpa?" Kyle turned to Petra. "About *any* of this? Did he ever say anything unusual?"

She'd been living here for at least a couple years now. She was the only person other than her mother and the ranch manager who'd spoken to him regularly.

"He just seemed like a nice old man," Petra said. "There wasn't anything you don't know yourselves."

"So unless someone's got a cell phone, we need to go back to the house and see if we can call him," I said. "Grandpa, I mean."

Petra shook her head, and I knew neither Kyle nor I had one.

"Yeah, good," Kyle said. He ran a hand through his hair. "Good, we'll do that."

We raced back to the house, Kyle outdistancing both Petra and me.

As my brother grabbed a phone in the parlor, I dashed to the basement. The lab books lay scattered on the desk, where Emma and I had left them last night.

I took a look at the Chronal Engine itself, at the dim round screen in the center that now looked brighter somehow. Then I looked closer.

A dot had appeared, with letters and numerals identifying it somehow. I copied them down on a scrap of paper.

The dot had to have been the active Recall Device. The Chronal Engine was tracking it somehow. And if I was reading it right, that meant Emma was about seventy or eighty million years in the past.

I wondered if there was a way to get the Chronal Engine to automatically bring the Recall Device back or if you had to activate the Recall Device manually.

I couldn't tell, though, and I wasn't going to randomly press buttons. And I certainly couldn't read the lab books that would tell me how.

After spending a moment looking for a key in the desk, I grabbed a bookend and smashed the locked glass case holding the Recall Device. I was just looking at how to set the coordinates on it when Kyle and Petra came thundering down the stairs.

"What was that?" he demanded, with a glance at the wreckage.

"It broke," I said. "How's Grandpa?"

Kyle shook his head. "Still unconscious."

I filled them in on the tracking lights.

"If we can't bring Emma back, then we have to go to her," Kyle said.

"Yes," I replied, holding up the Recall Device.

"Can you set it?" Kyle asked.

"I think so," I replied. "I was just trying."

"Good." Kyle took a deep breath. "We're going to need wheels. So what do we take with us to the land of the dinosaurs? An armored personnel carrier?"

"Well," Petra said, "there is a Hummer in the garage." She shrugged. "A VW, too."

"What?" I asked with a quick glance at my brother. "You mean a Beetle? A Bug?"

"A Bug," Kyle repeated, and told Petra what Grandpa had said.

She nodded. "Mr. Pierson had this all planned." A glint in her eye gave me a chill. "Come on!"

Kyle raced after her. Grabbing the Recall Device, I followed as she led the way out of the basement and across the lawn to the garage.

Flinging the side door open, she turned on the lights.

"We take the Bug," she repeated, with a gesture.

Sitting in the center of the garage, next to a black Hummer and a bass boat on a trailer, was a brand-new lime-green Volkswagen Beetle, with one of those after-market roof racks that are for bikes or surfboards or ordinary luggage.

This one already had packs tied down with blue nylon rope.

A sheet of paper was taped to the driver's-side window. It contained a typed inventory list of what had been packed on the roof and in the trunk.

Also, handwritten, was a note that read, "Take whatever else you think you'll need, but don't take the Hummer."

"Why not take the Hummer?" Kyle asked. "It's bigger."

"It's bad for the prehistoric environment?" I guessed.

Then I remembered some of the sketches in the lab books. On one of the French pages, there was a diagram that showed a field of some kind, centered around the Recall Device. "It's too big, I think. The chronal field, or whatever it's called, won't go around the whole thing, so we need to take something smaller."

"Good," Kyle said. "Let's go."

"What? *Now?*" I asked. "We need to check out the equipment and figure out how the Recall Device works, and we've got all the time in the world on this end."

Kyle looked at me like I was an idiot. "You said the Chronal Engine tracks the Recall Device?"

"Yeah, so we're good—"

"What if Emma and it aren't in the same place?" Kyle said.

He was right. The man could drop Emma off somewhere— anywhere in time—and then take off alone. Or, knowing Emma, she could've already gotten away from him. But she'd be lost with no way home. We needed to move quickly. "You guys check the supplies. I'll set up the Recall Device."

Back in the workshop, I could still see the dot representing the kidnapper. The numbers were still the same as those I'd written. I hesitated over the books. Even if I could've read them, bringing them back in time with us seemed risky. But what if we needed them?

There might be something we could decipher.

The thing is, I don't like instruction manuals. They're usually badly written, even when they're in English. In this case, though, it seemed a worse idea to leave them behind. I ran upstairs and grabbed my school backpack.

After a moment's consideration, I grabbed my laptop computer. After booting it, I went online and downloaded a couple freeware translation programs and copies of the Russian and Japanese alphabets.

Back downstairs, I shoved the lab books into the backpack with the computer. I hoped that the microfiche reader next to the card catalog meant that Grandpa had made copies.

I set the Recall Device, then ran out to see the VW parked right outside, Petra and Kyle standing next to it.

"Grandpa packed us clothes," Kyle said.

"What?" It seemed like such a bizarre thing for him to say, and Emma was the one who usually was concerned about what to wear.

"In our sizes," Petra added.

I looked into the pack Kyle held out. Two sets of clothes that were essentially identical to what I was wearing. T-shirts, socks, underwear, cargo shorts. There was also a rain poncho like the ones they give you at SeaWorld. I was already wearing hiking shoes.

"Look over the list," Petra said. "We couldn't think of anything he'd missed."

A compound bow and a recurve bow and two sets of broadhead arrows (Petra could use one, and Kyle had learned to use one back in his *Lord of the Rings* phase a couple years ago before he made starting wide receiver and got cool and he didn't really like to talk about it); four hunting knives; a multi-tool; a composite hatchet; a tent; granola bars; water purification tablets; matches; two flint and steel sets; three canteens; a first-aid kit including bandages and aspirin and antibiotic ointments; binoculars; flashlights; a small mirror; and cooking implements.

Compared to my mother, Grandpa had packed light.

"Camera?" I asked.

"Broken," Petra answered. "It fell on a rock."

Then the list looked okay to me.

"So we're ready?" I said.

"*I'm* ready," Kyle said. "Give me the Recall Device."

"What?" Petra and I demanded at the same time.

"I'm going," Kyle said. "Alone."

"Since when?" I put in.

He ran a hand through his hair. "Since now. Look. I've been thinking about this. It's too dangerous. I can't help Emma if I have to take care of you two."

"You don't have to 'take care' of me, city boy," Petra said, her back stiff.

"Me, neither," I said. As his jaw was starting to set in his "I'm Kyle, I'm stubborn" look, I went on. "Quick. *Pachycephalosaurus*. Friend or foe?"

"What's a . . . a . . . pachy . . . ?" he asked.

"Exactly," I replied, but I could see he wasn't convinced. "Look, I think we all have to come. Or else why would Grandpa have packed our clothes?"

It was true I wanted to go. But more than that, I felt like I *needed* to go. The only way Kyle and I were going to rescue Emma was by sticking together.

But part of me also wondered if we were being set up. What would happen if we didn't take the path that had been neatly arranged for us? If only Kyle went, would we lose Emma? Did we really have a choice?

Kyle was silent a long moment. "Fine."

But there was one more thing. Even if Grandpa had meant for Petra to go, it didn't seem fair to drag her into this. Whatever "this" was.

"Look," I said. "Kyle's kind of right. Emma's our sister. You don't have to come."

"Are you kidding? You were right the first time. Besides, I like Emma," Petra said. "And it's going to be a heck of an adventure."

"No wonder you two got along so well," Kyle muttered.

"Okay, then." I shifted the strap on my backpack. "Who's driving?"

< 40 >

Kyle was still a year away from his learner's permit.

"I am." He held up the keys. "It's an automatic transmission. A monkey could drive it."

"Good thing we've got one," I said.

When he punched my shoulder, I didn't even flinch. "I call shotgun."

Petra snorted. "Speaking of which, do y'all think it might be a good idea to bring firearms? I don't suppose either of you knows how to use a shotgun? Or rifle?"

At our startled glances, she sighed. "Oh, that's right, y'all're from *Austin*. Well, I don't suppose there's time to teach you enough to do any good. And we won't be able to find any good buckshot a hundred million years ago, anyway."

We climbed into the car. I set the Recall Device in the cup holder and checked the setting. Then it occurred to me. "Wait. This is a time machine, right? Why don't we just go back to earlier and stop her from going?"

"Because we didn't," Kyle answered.

"And your grandfather wouldn't have prepared all this if that was going to work, would he?" Petra asked.

It made sense. Still, I hesitated.

"Do it, Max," Kyle said.

I pressed the activation button.

We'll be back in no time, was my last thought before the flash of light.

AND THE REST IS PREHISTORY . . .

AND THEN WE WERE FALLING. AFTER ABOUT HALF A SECOND, WE hit the ground. The car bounced once and then came to a halt, facing a tree, tilted nose downward.

"Everyone okay?" Kyle asked, his voice shaky.

"Are you kidding? It *worked*," I answered. "The time machine worked!"

The three of us whooped and high-fived.

"Come on!" I said. I swung my door open and bolted out, promptly tripping down the small mound the car was perched atop. I climbed to my feet, aware of some slimy goo on my hands, and took a moment to look around.

I was sweating. It was hot and steamy, like summer on the Gulf Coast, but there was a moist, peaty smell on top of it, as well as the smell of the ocean. I pulled at the neck of my T-shirt to fan myself while Petra got out of the car, an arrow loosely nocked to her bow.

"Watch that, Robin Hood," Kyle said as he came around the front of the car.

The Beetle rested at an angle on a mound, nestled against a giant tree, at least a hundred feet tall, at the edge of a forest of other giants—redwoods, I thought—some with trunks as much as ten feet in diameter. The undergrowth seemed to be mostly ferns, with occasional stands of stubby palms and cycads.

Away from the forest was a sandy beach, about seventy-five, maybe a hundred feet wide, leading up to an endless expanse of glassy, still water.

Offshore, in the distance, a pair of islands broke the sea's surface, and sea birds soared overhead. I squinted, trying to make them out better, then heard the shrill cry of an animal from deep in the forest and became aware of the buzzing and chirping of insects. I slapped at a mosquito on my arm before it could draw blood.

"This is amazing," Petra said, staring up into the trees. "Like Endor, from *Return of the Jedi*."

"The Forest Moon," I corrected, out of habit. "Endor was the gas giant."

"Emma!" Kyle shouted, startling us both. *"Emma!"*

When we looked at him, he shrugged. "It was worth a try."

There was no answering shout.

I hoped we'd set down in a time and location near my sister, but there was no way to check, to be sure. I moved to wipe sweat off my face, then remembered the goo on my hand.

I wiped it off on my pants and crouched near the VW's right rear wheel, to see where it had come from, while Petra peered under the front.

We'd landed on a nest or something, but I couldn't see exactly what it belonged to. The car had completely crushed it. Whatever it was, it was feathered and about the size of a swan.

As I was reaching for a stick to prod the creature with, I heard a cry from Petra.

When I looked up, she was cradling a small, damp, feathered something in her hand. It cheeped.

"You dropped a car on its nest," Petra said, glaring from me to Kyle, "and killed its mother."

"Sorry." Kyle shrugged and looked closer. "Umm . . . why does it have teeth?"

I reached to grab one of its legs between thumb and forefinger to inspect its claws.

"It has teeth," I told him, releasing the chick, "because it's a dromaeosaurid dinosaur and they all had teeth."

"A what kind of dinosaur?" Petra asked.

"It's a dromaeosaur, like *Velociraptor*," I said, figuring she'd get the *Jurassic Park* reference. "You can tell from the retractable switchblade claw."

Among other things. Like the feathers and the teeth.

"So we made it to where we wanted to be?" Kyle asked.

It was a good question. So far as I could tell, from the creature

Petra was holding and from the trees and the cycads and the fact that there were little white flowers on the shrubby plant Kyle was trampling, the answer was yes. The problem with that, though, was that the Cretaceous had lasted millions of years, and we were trying to find an exact instant. "Maybe."

"So . . ." Kyle began.

"We're going to find her," I said.

In the meantime, Petra was cooing over the dromaeosaur chick, which, coming from a girl who shot bunnies with pointed sticks, seemed a little weird.

"What do these eat?" she asked, then apparently had a thought. She was crouched again, before I could answer, reaching under the car. "How about this?"

Petra held a cracked egg in her hand.

When I nodded, she set it by the front tire and put the chick down next to it.

The hatchling sniffed at the egg, circled it, gave a contented chirp, and then began eating its dead sibling. Which meant it was able to fend for itself as soon as it hatched. Dromaeosaurs *were* "precocious"—it was the sort of thing paleontologists would love to know. The sort of thing Mom would love to know.

I tried not to think about how she'd react to our being here.

About Emma being here.

"So what do we do now?" I asked, taking a step that seemed strangely unstable.

< 45 >

The hatchling sniffed at the egg, circled it, gave a contented chirp, and then began eating its dead sibling.

"Wait." Petra peered around. "Is the ground shaking?"

We looked from one to the other, as the next jarring sensation hit.

"Earthquake?" Kyle asked.

"Or volcano." I stood and walked toward the beach, past a cluster of ferns and a single, foot-high plant with four tiny white flowers.

Away from the canopy of redwoods, the heat felt more intense, like July in Texas, and the nearly cloudless sky was a brilliant shade of blue I'd never seen before.

"Not an earthquake," I said, pointing, as the others came onto the beach.

Striding toward us was a herd of giant sauropod dinosaurs. Greenish gray, wrinkled, their scaly hides shimmered in the sun. Their long necks were held angled above the ground, more vertical than horizontal, the heads of the largest thirty or so feet up.

Birds flew above them, occasionally alighting on the sauropods' sides and backs.

The herd strode about three or four across, the smallest ones toward the center of the group, their tails whipping back and forth.

It was amazing, like seeing the beginning of the world. Which, in a way, we were. Plants and animals had just started to take on their modern forms, and the continents were almost in their present locations.

And some of the animals were the size of houses.

With every step, the ground shook.

"Brontosauruses," Kyle said.

"There's no such thing as—" I began, then stopped.

The proper name, according to the rules set by the International Code of Zoological Nomenclature, was *Apatosaurus*. But I'd always *liked* the name *Brontosaurus*. "Thunder lizard" was way cooler than "deceptive lizard." And, okay, this was the Late Cretaceous, not the Jurassic, so these would be some kind of titanosaur like *Alamosaurus* and not a diplodocid apatosaur, anyway, but still.

I was here first.

So, thumbing my nose at the ICZN, I said, *"Brontosaurus* is fine."

We all went silent, watching the sauropods approach.

Then I gagged at the sudden stench. The wind must have changed. And what the books and fossils didn't tell you was how much the things *smelled*. Like every putrid odor at the zoo put together with a feedlot and an overripe cat box.

"Maybe we should get out of their way," I said.

We moved back under the cover of the redwoods.

When the baby dromaeosaur chick trotted to her, Petra scooped him up and placed him on her shoulder. He gave a contented peep and then nuzzled her hair.

"I think he imprinted," she said. "Like a baby bird."

I found the whole thing slightly unnerving.

Kyle asked, "Aren't you afraid he'll grow up and eat you?"

"They're animals, not monsters," Petra replied.

"And he'll grow up to be a lot smaller than the movie velociraptors," I put in, "so a full-grown human wouldn't have much to worry about, unless they were in a pack. A toddler, though, might—"

"Shut up, Max!" Kyle said.

I did, because by that point even I realized I was babbling.

"I think I'll call him 'Aki,'" Petra said.

"What's 'Aki'?" I asked.

"The name of my old shooting team coach's dog," she replied.

Kyle and I exchanged a look but said nothing.

By now the herd of brontosaurs was getting closer, almost alongside us. I took a step toward them. I could've walked underneath the creatures with room to spare. Even the little ones were twice the size of the VW.

Then the stench made me cough again.

I tried to not breathe through my nose, but that just made me think about what I was breathing in through my mouth. You could almost taste the smell, which was never good.

I was about to mention this when Petra's eyes widened. "Do not make any sudden moves," she said, "but get in the car now!"

I whirled and froze.

It was a full-grown tyrannosaur. Probably *T. rex*. The largest carnivore to have ever walked North America. The size of a city bus.

And it was coming toward us.

It hadn't seen us yet, though. It was stalking the sauropod herd from under the cover of the giant redwoods.

About fifteen or twenty feet tall, its scarred, scaly body was a mottled brown and green with vague tiger stripes.

Its huge mouth, with its battery of dagger-like teeth, was poised terrifyingly open. Its tiny two-clawed forearms looked a lot less goofy in real life.

Petra raised her bow and aimed an arrow, but then abruptly lowered it. "Like using a toothpick against a tiger."

"Move it!" Kyle said.

Petra scooted to the passenger side of the Bug and climbed in the back.

I scrambled in and slammed the door.

Kyle was in the driver's seat a moment later, the ignition on. "Where to?"

The car was facing a redwood, and the only way to go was back toward the tyrannosaur.

"Idiot!" Petra said. "Use the Recall Device."

I didn't have time to feel sheepish.

I grabbed the Device and pressed the activation button.

And nothing happened.

"Do it!" Kyle yelled.

"I did!" I yelled right back. "It's not working!"

Kyle reached over and slapped at the button.

< 50 >

Nothing happened.

"Guys," Petra said, "get us out of here. *Now.*"

The tyrannosaur had come closer, within maybe two or three body lengths, and the brontosaurs were striding past.

"It's not working!" Kyle said.

And then the tyrannosaur saw us.

We couldn't go through it. It probably weighed five tons. Its teeth were the size of bananas, and it could probably swallow any of us whole.

We had to get it out of the way.

I leaned over, grabbed the key chain dangling from the ignition, and pressed the alarm button.

The car's lights began blinking on and off, and a siren sounded.

Kyle gave me a horrified look. "What did you do?"

I didn't reply. The tyrannosaur paused at the unfamiliar sound.

Then, with a roar, it thrust its snout forward, prodding the packs on the roof of the car. The entire vehicle shifted, but the ropes held. Score one for modern technology.

A moment later the tyrannosaur raised its head again, snarled, and looked to the side. Toward the sauropods.

To our right, two of the largest stood facing the car and the tyrannosaur. They stamped their legs, shuffling back and forth, snorting and bobbing their heads.

Then the one on the right reared up and stamped its forelegs with a titanic crash that shook the ground.

The Beetle fishtailed once on the sand, then got traction, but not before it nearly sideswiped the largest of the brontosaurs.

The tyrannosaur roared once more, then straightened, hissed, and trotted away into the forest.

I leaned back and let out a breath as Kyle turned off the alarm, the adrenaline high draining away with the ringing in my ears.

"What about them?" he asked, pointing out the passenger window at the hostile sauropods.

"Drive!" I yelled.

Kyle slammed the car into reverse, hauled the wheel to the left, and then drove forward. Toward the herd.

"What are you doing?" Petra yelled.

I gripped the dashboard as Kyle maneuvered the car between the tree line and the sauropods. The Beetle fishtailed once on the sand, then got traction, but not before it nearly sideswiped the largest of the brontosaurs.

A moment later the car accelerated safely past the herd, although one whiptail clanged against the side sheet metal.

< 53 >

ON THE MOVE

"WHY DIDN'T THE RECALL DEVICE WORK?" KYLE ASKED.

"I don't know," I replied.

"How are we going to get back?" he asked.

"I don't know," I said again.

"How are we going to find Emma?" he pressed.

"Shut up and let me think." I grabbed the Recall Device from out of the cup holder. I checked to make sure it was set to "Return" and tried to activate it again.

Nothing.

Suddenly, I was glad I had brought the lab books.

Replacing the Recall Device, I pulled out the top book, the one in English, and began leafing through it.

At that moment Aki jumped into my lap, crumpling the page, and then sniffed at the lab book. He didn't seem hostile or afraid, just curious.

"Sorry," Petra said as I handed him back to her.

"Is that the instruction manual?" Kyle asked. "Because, you know, you're terrible with—"

"Shut up," I told him again, and tried to read.

Maybe the Recall Device needed to recharge.

Every now and then, I'd glance out the window. We were driving along a beach. I'd never been a fan of beaches. They were often full of sand, seaweed, and volleyball players.

"Nice beach," Petra said.

This one was a little different from the beach at Corpus Christi, though, mainly due to the footprints and the nature of the garbage.

Instead of the tracks of spring breakers going off to windsurf or bask in the sun, these were the enormous prints of giant sauropods. Along with gargantuan, fly-covered and beetle-infested steaming piles of dung. "Coprolites" they were called, after seventy million years of fossilization, when they were just like any other sedimentary rock and no longer smelled.

At least we were free of the tyrannosaur and the sauropod herd.

Although I was thinking we had bigger problems.

Aki chirped, and then Petra shifted in her seat behind me. "Do you have any idea how to find your sister and get us home?"

"Yeah," I said, more confidently than I felt. "Maybe. No."

"What's that?" Kyle asked.

"What's—" I began. I leaned forward, reaching out a hand to steady myself on the dashboard. Then I saw what he was driving toward. "Is that a boat?"

Neither of the others said anything as we approached and the boat came into clearer sight. Once, it had been a trim, white wooden river launch, about thirty feet long, with an exposed boiler and a single smokestack in front and a small cockpit behind it, sort of like the *African Queen* (from my mother's favorite movie). Now, half buried in the sand, front end pointing inland, it was resting at an angle, tilted on its right side. Bent and broken supports and tattered pieces of dirty white canvas showed where a canopy behind the cockpit had been. Clumps of dried seaweed lay gathered on the ground against the peeling hull. Much of the back end was missing.

A white and gray gull-like bird, perched at the bow, gave a cry and flew away at our approach.

I twisted in my seat to look as Kyle drove around the side of the boat. The hull had a four-foot hole at the front and just at the water line.

I tried to see inside, but the angle was bad.

"What do you think?" Kyle asked as we circled. "Does it look like something the kidnapper guy might've brought?"

"Maybe," Petra put in, "but it could also be something Pierson brought."

"Or sent," I said. "This could be what happens if you try to send something too big."

"Now there's a cheerful thought," she muttered.

"Stop here," I said as we drove into the boat's shadow. I pulled open the glove compartment for a flashlight. It was one of those expensive black aluminum kinds like the police use. Almost before the car had stopped, I jumped out.

Petra was out after me, Aki on her shoulder.

"What are you looking for?" Kyle asked, emerging from the driver's side.

"Something," I said. "I don't know. I just want to take a look. It's a boat from the twenty-first century. Or maybe the twentieth."

He banged a hand on the hood of the car. "How does this help us find Emma?"

"It's a *boat* in the Cretaceous," I repeated. "What do *you* think?"

Obviously, it had something to do with the Chronal Engine.

In the direct sun, the heat shimmered off the sand. I took the flashlight and went around to the other side of the boat.

After a moment Kyle and Petra followed.

I peered closer and saw that what I'd taken for odd wind patterns in the sand were instead hundreds of overlapping three-toed footprints.

The tracks were just a little larger than my hand. They were amazingly *real*. Not that the ones down at the ranch weren't cool, too. Those were bigger. But these were fresh, not fossils.

I gave Aki a glance, then became aware that Kyle was staring at him.

"Three-toed biped," I said, "means a theropod, but not a dromaeosaur. They only leave two toe marks, because they hold the one off the ground."

The switchblade one. The one that could disembowel you and leave your intestines on the outside so they could eat you at their convenience while you watched.

I didn't say this aloud, though, because sometimes you don't have to tell everyone everything.

Kyle came up beside me when I approached the boat, pointing my flashlight at the hole. "Hold the light from underneath," he said, "with your arm up. That way you can swing it down like a club." It was his "don't be a dork" tone.

I was tempted to snap at him that I wasn't an idiot, but decided not to, partly because what he'd said made a lot of sense. I braced myself, then shined the flashlight, holding it from below, and peered in.

Without warning, a slim, two-legged dinosaur jumped out of the hole.

I jumped back and stumbled into Kyle as the animal made a loud screeching noise, spreading its arms and lowering its head, trying to scare us off.

I kept my eye on it, though, even as I tumbled to the ground on top of Kyle.

The dinosaur was about five feet tall, covered in bright red and green feathers, and had long, feathered arms ending in claws. It also had an odd, chicken-like crested head and a giant, parrot-like beak, which meant it was an oviraptorid of some kind.

"Watch it!" Kyle said, grabbing the flashlight so I wouldn't jab him again, and scrambled to his feet.

At that, the oviraptorid squawked, turned, and ran off toward the forest.

"What was that?" Kyle reached out a hand. "Some kind of pre-historic parrot?"

"Oviraptorosaur," I answered, letting him pull me up. "They're mostly harmless. Except for the ones that are the size of a giraffe." I paused, considering. "Of course, those are from Mongolia . . ."

Petra chuckled, standing a few steps back with her bow at the ready.

"What?" I asked.

"Let's just say y'all need to work on your reflexes," she answered. "And you'd make terrible hunters."

After a moment Kyle gestured. "Let's check this thing out." He shined the flashlight into the hole again.

I couldn't see anything moving, so I took a step closer, this time sticking my head in and wrinkling my nose against the dead shell-fish smell.

It was just a small compartment, for storage, I guessed, with a rotting wooden deck above and broken doors leading to where the steam engine stood.

From the beam of light Kyle was using to scan the floor, I could make out eggshells and broken ammonite shells and the remains of what looked like small turtles.

"Are those from baby oviraptorosaurs or what the oviraptorosaurs ate?" Kyle asked.

"Possibly both," I replied. "A lot of dinosaurs may have been cannibals."

Like Aki, but I didn't say that aloud.

We stood and walked back the length of the hull, to stand next to the cockpit. I looked through the broken glass to see a pair of cracked gauges and a ship's wheel set into a weathered dashboard.

As I climbed up and made my way around to the stern, Kyle said, "Watch your step."

"Wait, what's that?" I asked.

He vaulted over the side to stand next to a corroded metal box, about a foot square, set into the deck just in behind the boiler. Then he crouched. As I made my way over, he pulled open a hatch on the box. Petra stayed behind, with her compound bow, watching from beside the boat.

"What is it?" I asked again.

He shined the flashlight into the compartment. "I don't know."

I moved closer. It was a rectangular collection of brass and glass and wiring, all wound together. Something inside was lit with a faint blue glow. Sticking up and off to the side was a series of dials with markings on them. The same markings I had on the Recall Device.

"A prototype, maybe? So Professor Pierson's original time machine was a boat?" I hadn't seen anything in the lab books about that. "Why would you build it into a boat?"

"Because he thought it was going to land in water?" Kyle speculated. "Do you think we can use this to get back?"

I shook my head. "I don't know. We need to find Emma first."

"Brilliant idea," he said. "Why didn't I think of that?" He gestured. "I don't suppose you have some clue where she might be?"

"No," I had to admit.

"Me, neither," Petra interjected before Kyle could say something else snide. "But I bet *they* do."

We stared back at her, but she was looking out to sea. Suddenly, she crouched and pointed. "Duck!"

"A boat!" Kyle said, dropping down so that he'd be hidden by the side of the launch.

And then I saw. Out at sea, maybe a mile down the shoreline, in the direction we'd been heading, was a boat. A launch, like the one we were on, only this one was whole and belching black smoke from its smokestack as it cruised parallel to the shore.

"Don't let them see you," Kyle said.

"You think they're the ones who took Emma?" I asked.

"Either that," Petra said, "or they can lead us to her."

I crouched beside her. From where the boat was, I figured the Beetle was hidden from their view. But there was a pair of binoculars in the trunk. Hoping I wouldn't be seen, I made my way over the side.

"Where are you going?" Kyle asked.

I ran to the car, grabbed the hatch handle, and yanked. And nearly pulled my arm off. It was locked. Because oviraptorids were prehistory's most notorious car thieves.

"Kyle!" I shouted. "Unlock the door!"

His face appeared above the side of the boat, looking startled. He pulled the keys from his pocket and pressed the button on the remote to release the hatch. I grabbed the binoculars.

I ran back to the wreck, looking out to sea where I'd last seen the steamer. "Where'd it go?"

Petra pointed. "Over there. It's heading toward the shore. I bet there's a river or inlet."

I peered through the binoculars and watched as the boat headed into shore and disappeared behind the trees and sand dunes that lay in front of us. The boat looked pretty much like the one we were standing on, but with fewer holes. The driver was obscured inside the cockpit, and I didn't spot any sign of anyone else. "If Emma's aboard, I don't see her."

Kyle grunted. "Well, we know enough to head upriver. Let's get a move on."

"Makes sense," Petra said.

"Hold on a sec." I jumped down from the boat and grabbed a notepad and pen from the car.

< 62 >

Then I scribbled a message on it, to Emma, if she ever made it here. That we were looking for her. Of course, knowing her, she was probably back already, feet up and relaxing.

We sealed the metal box in the deck as best we could. Maybe Kyle was right and we could use it to get home. But if it worked, why had it been left here to rot?

We climbed out of the boat and got into the car, Petra in the back as I took the shotgun seat again.

The second volume of the lab books rested at my feet while I held the first one open against the dashboard and tried to read.

"Drive," I told Kyle. "Don't get us lost. Oh, and try to find some fresh water."

Kyle looked at me like I was dense, but he drove. At least now we had kind of an idea where we were going, and there was a chance Emma was here.

It was a bit easier reading in the car than it would've been outside, since we had the air conditioner going, although the motion was giving me a bit of a headache. Or maybe that was the dehydration.

I took a swig from one of the canteens and directed the air vent at my face.

I wasn't really sure whether the a/c was a good use of the gas, but I wasn't going to complain right now.

Kyle drove us farther down the beach while I continued to read.

After a while I gave up on trying to figure out the lab books. The first one didn't seem to have anything helpful. The equations in all four were impossible, and for the foreign language stuff, I was going to have to break out the translation programs on the laptop.

And, honestly, I was feeling kind of nauseated because of the hills that Kyle kept driving us over. Finally, though, he brought the Bug to a halt at the top of a sand dune, overlooking the mouth of a river. Sandbars dotted the entrance, but at least one channel in the middle looked deep enough for a boat.

"Upriver," Petra said from behind.

Kyle nodded, then put the car back in gear and headed into the forest, trying to keep within view of the muddy brown water.

As we moved deeper into the forest, we also began going slightly uphill. Farther on, the VW mowed down waist-high ferns, as Kyle drove between giant redwood trunks and swerved to avoid half-buried, ancient logs.

Not long after we entered the forest, he reached down and turned on the radio. There was only static.

"Are you trying for the Greatest Hits of Seventy Million B.C.?" I asked. "Because it might be better to open a window."

He gave me a dirty look and switched the band to AM.

"The kidnapper could have an accomplice, and they could have radios," he said.

Which made a certain amount of sense, I guess.

But the scan setting on the radio didn't pick up anything.

After a moment I turned it off.

As we drove, I tried to keep a watch on the water, but didn't have a good view from the passenger seat. The river wound, and Kyle didn't exactly follow every twist and cutback, but we kept close enough that the muddy water was in sight most of the time.

I occasionally got a peek of something flying through the trees, but I couldn't tell if it was a bird, some new pterosaur, or maybe even a *Microraptor*. I wasn't sure whether those ever lived in North America, though.

Petra had scooted over, behind Kyle, so she could keep an eye out.

Suddenly, we turned a corner around a tree into a sort of clearing. Kyle slammed on the brakes and took a hard right. The VW stopped at the brink, about three or four feet from the edge of the embankment.

It wasn't high enough to really be a cliff, just a sloping rise overlooking the bottom of a *U* in the river, about ten or so feet below.

Trees grew, roots exposed, out of the water near the riverbank. Cypresses and maybe dawn redwoods. It felt a lot like the heights by MoPac Expressway, overlooking Lady Bird Lake in downtown Austin. At least that's what it could've been except for the giant alligators basking on the opposite riverbank.

As I pointed, one of the reptiles pushed itself up and slid into the water.

"Maybe one of those put that hole in the boat back there," Petra said.

"Maybe," I answered. These alligators *were* huge—thirty-five, maybe forty feet long. They had to have been *Deinosuchus*, one of the biggest alligators ever. Supposedly, they ate turtles, fish, and whatever else they felt like, including dinosaurs.

Kyle released his seat belt and opened his door to step out.

"Wait," I said, grabbing his arm. "What's that?"

I heard strange hooting and a noise vaguely like thunder.

The air freshener hanging from the rearview mirror began to shake, and not from the breeze.

Petra looked back toward the redwood forest. "We've got to get out of here."

I took a quick glance behind us and saw what I hadn't noticed before: cutting across the twists in the river, we'd been driving for a while on what looked like a path, about three or four car widths wide.

"What is it?" Kyle asked, but he closed the door and pulled his seat belt back on.

"Something's coming," I replied. As a precaution, I grabbed the Recall Device out of the cup holder and stowed it in my backpack with the lab books and laptop. "Drive!"

I'd just zipped the bag shut and Kyle had just put the key back into the ignition when the herd of dinosaurs plowed into us. The car lurched sideways, metal crumpling and glass shattering, as a massive body broadsided us.

Giant, hammer-headed hadrosaurs. Duck-bills. Brown and

green bodies, but with five-foot-long, bright blue and red crests that stuck out from the backs of their heads. *Parasaurolophus.* They were as large as elephants, which made me realize just how tiny a VW Beetle actually was. "Hang on!"

Kyle pressed the accelerator. I heard the engine rev, and we lurched forward. Then we were struck again. The right side caved in, and I felt my door, or maybe the entire frame of the car, press up against me.

The next thing I knew, Kyle yelled something, and the car was going over the edge of the embankment. My stomach lurched as we fell and grazed the side of a tree. A moment later the car splashed into the water and came to a rest on the driver's side, wedged between the roots of a cypress and the riverbank.

Then I dropped into ice-cold water on top of Kyle, and Aki screamed.

"Get off me!" Kyle managed to say through gritted teeth.

I struggled to get upright and saw Petra in the back trying to do the same. At the same time, I tried to keep the lab books and computer out of the water.

The water didn't stop rising until it was about three feet deep, which was enough to submerge nearly half the car.

My shoulder seemed a little bruised and my right ankle was throbbing, but other than that, I seemed healthy. "Everyone okay?"

"Yeah," Kyle replied, although his face looked white.

"Me, too," Petra said.

The car lurched sideways, metal crumpling and glass shattering,
as a massive body broadsided us.

I let out a breath. "Good."

In a few minutes, and with only a few more bruises, we managed to get ourselves upright and at least mostly out of the water.

"Gator!" Petra shouted, as I was hoisting myself out of the shattered passenger-side window. I watched, motionless, as the *Deinosuchus* approached the tree the car was caught on. Only the six-foot-long head of the gator was visible above the water. Three or four other trees closely surrounded the one we were caught in, so probably the *Deinosuchus* couldn't get right at us, but I still kept an eye on it.

After too long a moment, the *Deinosuchus* flicked its tail, roiled the water, and was gone.

"Stay on this side of the trees," Petra warned.

"Not a problem," I muttered as I climbed up to stand on the car frame. From where I was, I could see up onto the riverbank, where the herd had attacked us.

"Are they still there?" Kyle called.

"No," I said, and tossed my soaking backpack ahead of me.

We'd gotten lucky. The car was totaled, but a bigger herd might've trampled us completely flat.

I took another careful look around. I didn't see any more hadrosaurs, though, so I gripped a root sticking out of the bank and hoisted myself up.

IN THE FORESTS OF THE NIGHT . . .

"HAND ME THE PACKS," I CALLED DOWN.

As Kyle and Petra began to gather our baggage out of the trunk and off the roof, I took a look around. The *Parasaurolophus* had gone, but there were plenty of footprints, piles of dung, and trampled ferns.

My backpack, with the journals and my computer, was soaked. We'd need to dry everything out, but now wasn't the time. We had to get our stuff together and get out of there. I didn't think the herd would be returning, but playing it safe was probably a good idea.

While I was doing this, Petra hoisted herself onto the side of the car, balancing Aki on her shoulder. When she climbed up, the dromaeosaur spread his fuzzy arms like wings and then leaped off as I reached to give her a hand. Then Aki shook his feathers and lay down in the sun next to my backpack.

"What now?" I called.

Kyle emerged from the car and began tossing packs and bedrolls up at me. I let most of them fall to the ground.

"We should get out of here," Petra said, "as quickly as we can."

"I know. We can't leave our supplies, though," I said.

"We can't take it all." She pulled a bandanna out of a pocket and wiped sweat off her forehead. "We're going to have to leave something."

"How much did Grandpa know?" Kyle asked as he climbed up to the bank and stood, stiffly, off balance. At my raised eyebrow, he continued, "Because if he knew everything, then wouldn't he have had us bring less junk?"

"Maybe," I answered. "Or maybe we have to choose. You okay?"

He took a deep breath, wincing, but lifted up the bottom of his T-shirt. His left side was covered in a purple and black bruise. "I'll live. What about the two of you?"

Petra had a cut over her eye and a few bruises on her arms and legs, but otherwise seemed all right. I had a nasty gash on my ankle and a bruised shoulder blade, but didn't think anything was broken.

I was a little worried about my brother, though. He'd gotten beat up a couple times like this playing football, and it usually required a lot of ice and sitting still. But if he didn't want to make a big deal about it, I wasn't going to.

We got off the game trail and quickly cleaned our cuts with the antiseptic from the first-aid kit and bandaged up the bigger ones. The gash on my ankle was about four inches long and deep enough that it would've freaked Mom into taking me in for stitches. The bleeding seemed to have mostly slowed to an ooze, though.

In the end, we found that the tent was torn, so we left that, but we packed the spare clothes, sleeping bags, fire-starting tools, knives, the hatchet, canteens, granola bars, first-aid kit, water purification tablets, flashlights, multi-tool, mirror, Petra's bow (the other one broke), and the arrows (some of which were bent). And my computer and the lab books. We tied the remaining supplies up a tree with rope.

When we were done, I unzipped an inner pocket of my backpack and pulled out a Ziploc bag of yogurt-covered raisins. I grabbed a handful, then held out the bag to Petra.

She took a few and I tossed the bag to Kyle, while she held a raisin out to Aki. The dromaeosaur sniffed at it, gingerly took it into his mouth, and gulped it down.

"Should he be eating those?" I asked, as Petra fed him another.

"Why not?" she replied, not looking up.

I couldn't think of a real reason—it just seemed bizarre that a dinosaur should eat a dairy product from the twenty-first century (were dinosaurs lactose intolerant?).

I was still contemplating the digestive tract of the juvenile dromaeosaur when I heard a roar in the distance.

"Maybe we should get moving," I said. "We should also probably find some kind of shelter for the night."

After about a couple miles or so of hiking, we found ourselves above a creek that fed into the river. We followed it upstream, away from the river, where the water ran clean. And we'd still have a view of any boats moving upriver. We made camp there, where a six-foot-wide redwood had fallen out to bridge the creek. Another tree lay propped on top of it, more or less parallel to the stream. Yet another stood next to both. It seemed like as good a shelter (Petra called it a "stockade") as we were going to get.

"We should be all right tonight," she said as we dropped our packs, "so long as the stream doesn't rise, in which case we'll be washed away and probably drown."

Kyle gave her a look. "We're, what, a good three or four feet above the water?"

"You ever seen a good old-fashioned central Texas flash flood?"

Kyle grumbled something I couldn't hear, so I decided not to bring up extreme possibilities like volcanic eruptions or the Chicxulub meteorite.

I slapped at a mosquito. "Let's get a fire going." It would keep carnivores at bay and, hopefully, insects, too. Also, the fire would dry out the lab books. And then we'd be able to find our way home. Once we got Emma back, that is.

The Recall Device should've put us down at the right time and place, but really, other than the brief blip on the tracker on the Chronal Engine, the only confirmatory evidence we had that she was here was those footprints back at the ranch.

And the thing was, to make a fossil, you needed something to bury the tracks. Like a lot of muddy water or a volcano. I just hoped she hadn't gotten caught in either.

Then there was the whole survival issue. I had never—and I do mean never—gone camping, and I knew too much about dinosaurs to really feel comfortable out in the relative open without, say, an M1 Abrams tank or something.

While Petra and Kyle prepared camp, I went off to look for firewood. The shadows were longer now, and the forest seemed filled with mysterious dark spaces. Although I couldn't see the sun anymore, it was still hot.

To be honest, at this point, I was kind of borderline terrified, but it was like there was so much to be scared about that all the individual frightening pieces seemed small.

We'd already seen tyrannosaurs and titanosaurs and dromaeosaurs and oviraptorids and hadrosaurs. What else could be lurking in the night?

At the same time, it was incredible that we were three of the only five human beings on the planet (that I knew of) and that it would be at least sixty-five and a half million years, and probably a whole bunch more, before any others appeared.

It was getting darker, so I quickly gathered dead wood and returned to the camp, where the others had already prepped a place for the fire, clearing dried fern fronds and cycad branches. I dropped my bundle of branches, wiped sweat off my face, and

< 74 >

swatted at mosquitoes, more out of habit than for hope of it doing any good.

Kyle knelt, shaving away at one piece of metal with another. Every time, a spark flew off the end, onto a small pile of fuzz that lay in front of him, on top of a dried cycad branch. The fuzz didn't ignite, though.

"Flint and steel," Petra said. "Either of you ever start a fire this way before?"

"No," Kyle said, "like I told you. But I've seen it done this way on TV." A drop of sweat fell off his nose. He leaned back, wiping his face with the bottom of his shirt, then waved away a mosquito.

"Tomorrow night's your turn," Petra told me.

"Joy," I replied.

She sat, resting back against a tree, looking a lot like she was enjoying herself. "Have a seat. We're going to be here awhile." Then, as I was sitting, she looked at the pile of wood I'd brought. "Actually, come on, we're going to need more than that."

For the next half hour, we gathered wood and brought it back to the campsite. And with each bundle of firewood, which Petra delivered with a cheerful whistle, Kyle's face got redder and redder. His jaw was clenched as he worked at starting the fire. Of course, his ribs couldn't have been feeling all that well, either.

On one of our outings, I found a stick about an inch thick and about as long as I was tall. I trimmed off the smaller branches so I could use it as a quarterstaff.

Friar Tuck vs. the *Velociraptor.* I decided I was more tired than I'd realized.

"You know, we could just use the matches," I finally whispered to Petra as we headed out one more time into the dark.

At this point we had way more firewood than we needed. And I was worried about the books. I didn't think their being wet a little longer would matter much, but I wasn't sure we should risk it.

"Maybe," she replied, grinning, as we went off again. "Why don't we give him a few more minutes?"

We headed off into the darkness until I was thoroughly lost, even with a flashlight, but Petra seemed to know where we were going.

"By the way," she said, "what's edible? If we have to be here awhile?"

"You think we're going to have to be here awhile?"

"Not to get all *Swiss Family Robinson*," she replied, "but pretend, for the moment."

I bent to pick up more sticks. "A lot of things. Some fir tree needles, but there probably won't be anything like modern fruits and berries—I mean, there'll be flowering plants, which means fruit, but I don't think there's anything like an apple or coconut yet. Maybe a fig or two." I shrugged. "I could be wrong. There *will* be small dinosaurs and mammals, though, if we can hunt and trap. Also, there are fish and crayfish and bugs."

A second later we heard a shout from the campsite.

"Fire!" Kyle cried.

Petra flashed a grin and then said, "Let's go."

She led the way back to the camp, which really wasn't difficult because by now there was a huge, flickering glow.

"Congratulations," I called when we came in sight.

"Yeah," Petra began. "How long did it take?"

I didn't really listen to the reply and didn't say anything further since tomorrow it would be my turn.

Though we didn't need the heat, the fire felt like home and safety.

Kyle was soaked with sweat, so he took a dip in the creek while I laid out the lab notebooks in front of the fire.

After a dinner of granola bars—Aki particularly liked the chocolate one—we decided to keep watch. At least, Petra suggested it, and Kyle and I agreed. It made sense, really. I mean, we were in a place where the predators could swallow you in one gulp and where *small* herbivores were bigger than hippos.

And the hippo was the deadliest animal in modern-day Africa.

Besides, there was a chance that we'd be able to spot that river launch if it headed back downriver.

< 77 >

So, deep into the night, I sat up on the log, listening to forest noises. The sounds were familiar, almost surprisingly so. The gurgle of the stream was a white-noise background to the buzzing of insects and the occasional calls of birds, or other arboreal creatures high up in the trees. There was a kind of deep, hooting noise from the river, which I figured was the *Deinosuchus*.

The moon was nearly full, but its light didn't really penetrate the shadows.

Once in a while, I heard something roaring from the forest that I hoped was farther away than it sounded, and every now and then, I had to brush away something crawling on my leg that I hoped even more wasn't a scorpion.

Occasionally, I heard a splash in the water, which I assumed was from fish or from something like a lizard going after the fish. Or it could have been from turtles or crayfish, since those predated the dinosaurs by millennia. At least, crayfish did.

I was contemplating what kind of fish there might be in the stream (yes, I was bored, but I was trying to stay awake) and had decided that there might be gars or coelacanths or freshwater sharks, but probably no trout or salmon. I didn't really know for sure because I'd never spent a lot of time reading up on freshwater Mesozoic fish because, well, fish are boring.

That's when I heard a low, throaty rumble from the edge of the clearing, off to my right. I slowly turned to look. At first I couldn't see anything, but then I heard the crack of a large branch.

< 78 >

I shined the flashlight in the direction of the sounds and then
let out a piercing yell. It was a tyrannosaur.

I scrambled to my feet on the log to face whatever was there.

I shined the flashlight in the direction of the sounds and then let out a piercing yell. It was a tyrannosaur.

A miniature version of what we'd encountered earlier. It stood about six feet high at the hips and its snout was relatively smaller and slimmer. Its markings were different, too: more spotted than striped. But it still had razor-sharp claws and a mouth so big it could easily bite a person's head off. And it was still bigger than a full-grown grizzly.

< 80 >

NIGHT WATCH

THE LIGHT CAUGHT THE TYRANNOSAUR IN MIDSTRIDE, ITS LEFT foot upraised.

The creature froze.

"What is it?" Petra was instantly awake and on her feet, grabbing the bow.

Kyle rolled over and came up standing, one hand holding on to the hatchet, the other on his ribs.

I yelled again, shining the beam of the flashlight into the tyrannosaur's eyes.

With a hiss, the creature turned and rushed off.

And then another mini-tyrannosaur emerged from the shadows and followed.

"What are those?" Petra began.

"Shhh!" I said, holding up my hand. I pointed the flashlight at the place in the tree line where the creatures had disappeared, and listened.

When I felt sure they were gone, I lowered the light and clicked it off.

I slid off the log and sat next to the fire.

< 81 >

Aki curled up next to Petra's bedding and went back to sleep.

"What were they?" she asked again.

"They looked like mini-tyrannosaurs. *Nanotyrannus*," I answered. Probably, although they could've been just juveniles of a bigger species. Like *T. rex*. Or *Daspletosaurus*. Or *Albertosaurus*. I didn't say anything more.

Kyle yawned, setting the hatchet down beside him. "If they come back, wake me up." With that, he rolled over, back to the fire.

Petra snorted. "Some people." She paced, her arms stretched out, then twisted her spine so that it made a cracking noise. "Is it my turn yet?"

I looked at my watch. "Yeah."

Without another word, she took the flashlight and climbed atop the fallen redwood log, her back against a root.

I was a little wired, so I thought I'd be awake for a long time, but ended up falling asleep almost immediately. When I awoke again, it was morning, the sky bright. I felt sore all over and had a sharp pain in my neck.

I stood and stretched, trying to get the kinks out. Petra was nowhere around. The fire had nearly died out.

And Kyle was sitting on the log in the same place I'd last seen Petra. His head rested on his arms, folded over his knees, his eyes closed.

For a moment I was annoyed—there was a reason we'd de-

< 82 >

cided to keep watch. There were a *lot* of reasons, and they involved many teeth and claws.

I was trying to decide what to do when I heard Petra emerge from behind a tree by the stream. She was holding a T-shirt in a bundle while Aki trotted behind her. As she came closer, I saw that she was carrying something in the bundle. Several somethings. One of them moved. Crayfish. About a dozen.

"Plenty more, too," she whispered as I gave her a thumbs up.

"Why are you whispering?" I asked, then realized I was whispering, too.

Petra gestured at my brother. "So we don't wake . . ." She stopped, realizing what she was saying. "Hey!"

She tiptoed over until she was right next to him.

"Don't even think about it," Kyle said, his eyes still closed.

Petra hit him in the arm. Hard.

"Ow!" he said, eyes opening, as he rubbed where she'd struck him, although I kind of thought he was overdoing it.

Then as Kyle started to swing his legs over to jump down, he slipped, toppled over sideways, and fell off to the far side of the log. His left hand slapped at the mossy bark, and he let out a yell as he went over.

I bit back a laugh and rushed to check on him—it was kind of a long drop.

When I leaned over the trunk, I saw that Kyle lay sprawled on his back, wincing, holding on to his side.

"You okay?" I said, remembering his ribs.

"Yeah—" Kyle began, then let out a cry and scrambled backwards.

A pair of small, brown, furry, slim-bodied creatures had emerged from the ground under the log and were making high-pitched barking noises at Kyle.

"They're adorable!" Petra said, peering over, as she raised a hand to settle Aki, whose downy feathers stood on end.

"They look kind of like rats," Kyle said. "Probably one of your ancestors, Max."

There was silence. Then Petra spoke. "You do realize, umm . . ."

I chuckled and didn't really listen to what Kyle said next. I was focused more on the creatures themselves. They were about the size of rats, with ratlike tails, but longer and slimmer, like someone had taken a squirrel, stretched it out, and shaved its tail. "They're probably multituberculates. Rodents didn't evolve until the Paleocene."

"What are multituberculates?" Petra wanted to know.

I hesitated. "They're kind of like rats. But their teeth are different."

At this Kyle snorted. He brushed dirt off the seat of his cargo pants and backed away from the creatures. When they were about ten feet away, they calmed and returned to their burrow.

"What's for breakfast?" Kyle wanted to know.

"Crayfish," Petra replied.

"We have crayfish?" he exclaimed.

"The creek has crayfish," Petra said with a grin. "Free range. Organic."

"All right!" Kyle clapped his hands, then rubbed them together. "Nothing quite like hunting crawdads in the morning to build me an appetite!"

With that the three of us descended into the stream, searching the mud, pulling up rocks and logs. It wasn't long before we managed to find several and tossed them into a pile on the creek bank. Not enough for a full, all-out boil, but enough that, with the granola bars, we wouldn't starve. At least not for another day.

As we regarded the pile of crayfish, Kyle looked thoughtful. "So, today we need to find the kidnapper's base of operations, rescue Emma, and figure out how to get out of here."

"Yeah," I said.

"Easy-peasy." Petra nodded.

"Good," Kyle replied. His stomach rumbled. "Anyone have any idea how we're going to cook these guys?"

In the end, we used the pot from the cooking kit and boiled the crayfish. It took a while, and the meal wasn't really as satisfying as back home, when you had a cast-iron cauldron, potatoes, carrots, corn on the cob, and a lot of cayenne pepper. But otherwise the meat tasted the same, which was something.

While Kyle and I ate the tails, Petra broke open some of the bodies and fed them to Aki.

The fuzzy hatchling studied each piece, batting it around and pouncing like a kitten, before finally eating it. I watched as the dromaeosaur stuffed himself.

"What are you going to do with him?" I asked.

Petra shrugged. "Train him. Maybe to hunt. You know, like a falcon."

"Just so long as he doesn't hunt us," my brother put in, then tossed the chick a crayfish head.

< 86 >

ON THE EDGE

IT WASN'T THAT DIFFERENT HERE THAN AT THE RANCH. WALKING upriver, I mean. It was hot and humid, and we were being eaten alive one tiny mouthful at a time by insects. The smells weren't that different either, and it was almost creepy how "normal" the plants looked. The ferns and cycads looked like the ones at the prehistoric garden in Zilker Park. Every now and then, we'd walk past a ginkgo.

The conifers were bigger, but this was, after all, a redwood forest.

It wasn't until you heard the cry of something in the distance that you realized you were on a wholly unfamiliar earth. An ancient place with sounds no human ear had ever heard and that had been silenced millions of years ago . . . That was a little unnerving.

So was the fact that the birds had teeth.

"So, we're here," Kyle said, turning to look at Petra and me. "Basically, we've got these dinosaurs bigger than elephants that want to eat us, dinosaurs the size of horses that want to eat us, dinosaurs the size of wolves that want to eat us, and other dino-saurs the size of elephants that want to trample us?"

"Pretty much," I said. "There are also some the size of ele-phants that could impale us with their horns and others the size of rhinos that could bludgeon us to death with their tail clubs. And it's possible there are giant pterosaurs that might be terres-trial hunter-scavengers that could also want to eat us. And if we go into the water, there are sharks and mosasaurs, as well as the big, giant alligators."

And almost all of the dinosaurian carnivores could take down any mammal with ease (other than maybe an *Indricotherium*, a rhino that was as big as a sauropod, but those wouldn't be around for another twenty or thirty million years).

Kyle grunted and led on.

We were alone, with only the barest minimum of supplies. And Emma had even fewer. Unless the guy who kidnapped her had a well-stocked camp.

We needed to find her and get home.

Which was fine, as far as it went. But something didn't fit. Why did the guy take Emma? If Grandpa had known about all this, why hadn't he tried to save her? Was she involved somehow in something that had to happen? Or was she going to be involved somehow?

Maybe some of the answers were in the lab books, but the

pages were still sticking together. And I was still afraid to try booting my computer.

I was just thinking that my next laptop should be one of those heavy-duty waterproof ones with the rivets that look like they're carved out of a single piece of steel, when we reached an area where the redwoods thinned and the sky on the forest side began to open up. The sounds of the beasts and birds and insects gave way to a low, steady roar.

Kyle began, "Sounds like a—"

"Waterfall," Petra finished.

We stepped into a clearing and onto a bank looking down about three feet into another creek channel. Unlike the last one, the channel wasn't full, but the creek that snaked its way across the bottom was still fast moving.

A rocky sandbar sat in the river at the mouth of the channel, with about a half dozen *Ichthyornis*—like toothed gulls—wading and occasionally darting their heads to pluck up a fish. About fifty feet upstream, the creek water foamed from a twenty-foot waterfall flowing over a terraced, rocky drop-off. Cypresses grew at the creek's edge, and rushes and horsetails grew on marshy soil to our right.

A small monitor lizard slithered from between a pair of ferns into the water.

"Very nice," Petra murmured. We clambered down the creek

bank, and she let Aki onto the ground. For a moment we paused at the edge of the creek, refilling our canteens and enjoying the feeling of coolness that came from the sound of the rushing water.

With a small sigh, Petra dropped her pack and sat on a log that lay partially buried, a few feet from the water's edge. She muttered something about blisters and then, with a cry, shot up, standing, brushing at her legs.

"What?" I asked.

"Scorpion!" She stepped away from the log, peering around it. Then, with one hand, she flipped the log up and pushed it aside.

The scorpion—about three inches long with a beige and black carapace—scurried out.

I moved closer to get a better look and caught sight of a pair of centipedes trying to burrow into the mud. Aki leaped after one, jabbing his snout into the dirt.

With a satisfied chirp, he came up with it, wriggling and flailing its legs.

Then Aki gulped the centipede down and began sniffing at the ground again. I couldn't see what he was looking for until he pounced and grabbed with his teeth. A thin, wet, rubbery shape stretched as it resisted his grip.

Finally, Aki stood straight, triumphant, the prey dangling from his mouth.

"Is that an earthworm?" Kyle asked.

I knelt, but not so close as to spook the little dromaeosaur. "Looks like it."

Aki's prey appeared to be a normal, ordinary, twenty-first-century, garden-style earthworm. About four inches long with a moist skin and segmented body.

With a couple snaps of his jaws, Aki finished it off.

Using my fingers like a rake, I ran a hand across the mud, pulling up another earthworm. It looked like every earthworm I'd ever found. They were edible and high in protein, my dad had told me once. Which was why people used them as bait for fish. "Lunch, anyone?"

Petra made a face while Kyle held out his hand. She and I exchanged a glance as my brother washed the worm in the clear water of the stream.

"You're not actually . . ." Petra began.

"I don't think we can afford to be picky," he murmured, as he held it by one end in front of him. *"Hakuna matata."*

He dropped the earthworm into his mouth like a strand of spaghetti. Then he grimaced as he swallowed.

I laughed and raised my hand to high-five when, suddenly, Aki squawked and raised his arms, looking across the narrow creek toward the rushes and the forest on the other side, where the creek met the river.

Instead of running into it, though, they jumped onto the vertical trunk and, flapping their arms, proceeded to run straight up.

An instant later a trio of small feathered dinosaurs—only about a foot and a half long—burst from the reeds and ran straight at the first of the cypresses.

Instead of running into it, though, they jumped onto the vertical trunk and, flapping their arms, proceeded to run straight up.

"Did you see that?" Kyle asked.

It was incredibly cool. The animals were probably some species of *Bambiraptor*, small relatives of Aki's. And what they'd just done was behavior scientists had speculated on, something seen in modern birds like partridges, called "wing-assisted incline running."

It was something they did to escape predators.

STRANGER ON A PLAIN

BEFORE I COULD YELL OUT A WARNING, THE FIRST OF THE HUNTING pack arrived.

A dromaeosaur, like Aki, only fully grown. It raced to the foot of the tree, then stopped, looked up, and snarled.

There was no response from the bambiraptors in the tree, but Aki hissed.

The lead dromaeosaur turned toward the sound as the rest of the pack arrived. Only four more, but they were still the size of Doberman pinschers, with vicious teeth and slashing claws.

Kyle brandished the hatchet while Petra raised her bow.

I stood ready with the quarterstaff. At the same time, I scanned the creek bank, trying to find a good spot to climb to safety.

"Five," Kyle said. "We can take five."

I wasn't so sure.

Petra sucked in a sharp breath. "How do you feel about nine?"

Four more dromaeosaurs joined the pack. Like the first five, they eyed us warily.

"We've got to—" I began, but was interrupted when Petra let loose with the bow.

The arrow hit the lead dromaeosaur in the shoulder, just above the arm.

It screamed and raced off. The others fled after it.

"It won't take long for it to bleed to death," Petra observed. "They good to eat?"

"You want to go after it?" I blurted.

She shrugged. "Be nice to get the arrow back."

"I don't know," I said, deciding not to raise the issue of whether it was a good idea to follow a pack of angry dromaeosaurs into unfamiliar territory or whether it was merely insane. "They're related to birds and alligators, so they could taste like either."

"Leave it!" Kyle said, looking at us like we were both nuts. He waded across the creek and up the other bank.

Petra and I followed, pushing through the horsetails and ferns growing in the mud until we were on solid ground again. It was bright in the sun, with fewer redwoods and more trees with waxy-looking leaves. (I don't know what kind. Trees are even more boring than fish.)

As I was about to speak, Kyle exclaimed, "They're back!"

I stepped forward to stand beside Kyle, Petra on the other side. Ahead of us, a pair of dromaeosaurs was picking at a six-foot *Triceratops* skull, horns angled into the air, surrounded by a haze of flies. The reddish-brown bones didn't have much meat left on them, the head frill and face scraped clean. The rest of the skeleton must've been dragged off long ago.

As we left the undergrowth, the dromaeosaurs looked toward us. Another three came around from the other side, approaching as if to challenge us.

Petra nocked another arrow just as a figure—a *human* figure—ran out from the forest toward the dromaeosaurs, yelling and brandishing what looked like a club.

Startled, the creatures took one look and then bolted away.

The guy stopped and turned toward us. "Well, that was fun! I don't suppose one of y'all is named Kyle?"

He was about our age, between Kyle and me in height and build. He wore a black cowboyish hat, khaki trousers tucked into black stovepipe boots, and a long-sleeved white shirt, sleeves rolled up. An old-fashioned backpack and quiver of arrows were strapped to his back, and a canteen hung from his waist. In one hand, he carried a recurve bow.

"I'm Kyle," my brother answered. "Who are you?"

The guy tipped his hat. "Samuel." He bowed. "Samuel Littleton, at your service." He gave Kyle an appraising look. "I think I have something for you."

"Do you have a Recall Device?" Petra blurted before I could stop her. For all we knew, this guy could've been in cahoots with the kidnapper.

Samuel blinked at her intensity. "I don't know what that means," he replied. "What's a Recall Device?"

"It's part of a time machine called the Chronal Engine," Petra answered. "We need one to return home."

"A time machine," Samuel said. "That explains a lot." He took off his hat and blotted sweat from his forehead with his sleeve. "It was either that or Conan Doyle's *Lost World*."

"How did you know Kyle's name?" I demanded. Something about the guy bugged me. He seemed way too calm—or maybe too smooth for someone in the current situation. Not to mention the fact that he was, for no apparent reason, here in the Cretaceous.

Samuel was silent a moment. "I have a message for him."

"A message?" Kyle said. "From who?"

Samuel hesitated again. "I don't know. Listen, y'all'd best come with me."

"You don't have a Recall Device?" Petra asked.

"No," Samuel replied. He gestured. "I don't know how I got here. My brother and I were out camping, then there was a flash of light, and I found myself here. In the middle of a pack of dinosaur lizards. That was ten days ago." He cocked his head as if listening. "But we can get to the bottom of that later. Right now, we need to go. I've got a camp just a spell upriver. Those vicious feathered things will be back soon."

His eyes widened as Aki emerged from Petra's hair. "Like that, only bigger."

"It's a baby dromaeosaur." Petra stroked Aki under his chin. "I'm training him."

Samuel gripped his bow with both hands. "If you want my advice, I would say to drown the little monster right now because you'll never be able to control him."

"Uh-oh," I heard Kyle mutter.

"I am *not* going to drown him," Petra snapped. "And if I wanted your advice, I would have asked for it."

After a tense moment, Samuel gave up. "Fine, then." He took a couple steps, then paused to see if we were with him.

With a shrug, Kyle began to follow.

"Wait." I grabbed my brother's arm. I lowered my voice. "Do you think this is a good idea?"

"No," he answered, "I think, other than the boat, this is our only lead."

Petra nodded, then strode after Samuel.

"What's your connection to Professor John Pierson?" I asked, as I stepped forward.

"Who?" Samuel said, giving me a blank look.

"The guy who invented the time machine," I replied. "We were at his place when we were sent here." I avoided looking at Petra and Kyle and hoped they would get the hint: we weren't going to tell this Samuel any more than necessary.

Samuel wiped sweat off his face. "I've never heard of anyone named Pierson."

< 98 >

"You didn't have anything to do with the boats?" Petra asked.

"What boats?"

As she explained about both the beached boat and the one we'd seen going upriver, I regarded the newcomer. "What year was it when you left?"

Samuel blinked. "It was 1919. And y'all?"

"Early twenty-first century," I put in. I didn't think it was smart to be telling Samuel about his future world. Potentially even his future. Who knew what that could do to the time stream?

"Why are y'all here?" Samuel said.

"We're here to rescue their sister," Petra answered, and explained about Emma's kidnapping.

"Oh." Samuel looked thoughtful. "Well, there's this hill near this cave I found. You can see for miles."

"That's . . . convenient," I said.

Almost too convenient.

"Where were you camping?" I asked.

"What?"

"You were camping with your brother, you said," Kyle put in. "Where?"

"Out," Samuel said with a slight hesitation. "Out along the Guadalupe River." He looked off into the forest, then back. "Listen, I know something strange is happening, but we have to get moving."

"Why?" Petra demanded.

"Y'all can trust me or not," Samuel replied, "but I told you . . . in addition to that vicious pet of yours, we're in the territory of a pride of *Tyrannosaurus rexes*. I've seen the footprints, and, believe me, we don't want to meet what made them face-to-face."

If he had been here awhile, he should know the territory at least a little better than we did. And if Samuel was telling the truth about the *T. rex* pride, we definitely needed to clear out. And since it was only recently that paleontologists concluded that tyranno-saurs might have traveled in prides, Samuel was likely telling the truth about that at least.

Assuming he really was from 1919.

< 100 >

Chapter
XI

MESSAGES

SAMUEL LED THE WAY, WITH KYLE RIGHT NEXT TO HIM. THEY WERE talking about how Samuel had survived here for so long. Or what Samuel claimed he'd done, anyway. It involved eating something called fiddlehead ferns and hunting a pair of small birds with stubby, one-fingered claws where their wings should've been. These sounded to me like alvarezsaurs, which were theropod dinosaurs, but actually fairly close to birds.

I didn't see any reason to tell Samuel or Kyle this, especially since they were now talking about Knute Rockne and the development of the forward pass in college football. After a few moments, I drifted back to hike beside Petra and tried to ignore the throbbing in my ankle from the cut.

"What's wrong?" she asked, her voice just above a whisper.

"I don't know," I answered, watching my step. "It just seems . . . Samuel's being here is awfully coincidental."

"Our being here seems awfully coincidental," she observed. "So's the fact that you're some kind of dino expert, and we happen to have been transported to the era of dinosaurs, but I don't think you sent us here."

I felt my face redden.

"You don't trust him?" she asked.

"I don't know," I said again. "But we're here to find my sister, and I think he's hiding something. And bringing a stranger with us could be dangerous."

Petra raised a hand for Aki to nuzzle. "It seems to me that we were mostly strangers, at least until two days ago."

"Sure, yeah. But our moms knew each other. And your mom works for my grandfather. So we're not exactly total strangers."

She smiled. "Just because Samuel is attractive and mysterious doesn't mean he's dangerous."

I could not believe she'd just said that. "You think he's 'attractive and mysterious'?"

"Not as cute as your brother, though. Maybe more mature."

"Wonderful," I said, deciding not to take the conversation any further.

"That doesn't mean I trust him, though," she finished.

For a while the only sounds came from our footsteps and the forest creatures. Birds and dinosaurs called in the distance. The river to our left meandered its muddy course downstream. I paused once or twice to take a look, but didn't see any *Deinosuchus*. Or steamboats. Or signs of Emma.

Every now and then, out of the corner of my eye, I would spot something scurrying in the trees. I couldn't tell if it was a bird, a dinosaur, or a mammal. I just didn't want it to drop on my head.

Not long after my talk with Petra, the trees thinned and the forest brightened. It wasn't what you would call sunny, because the sky was cloudy and it looked like rain, but there was definitely more light.

At the edge of a clearing stood a fifteen-foot-tall stump, about ten feet in diameter, the remains of a redwood that had fallen or rotted away or maybe had been struck by lightning. Beside it were ashes from a campfire.

Samuel hoisted himself into a cleft in the side of the stump. He tossed a bag out at me.

A modern grocery bag made from recycled material. From Whole Foods.

"I don't believe it," I said, peering inside.

"What is it?" Kyle wanted to know.

I pulled out a package of stiff blue material. It unfolded as I held it up. It was some kind of body armor. A bulletproof vest. Kevlar, I supposed. Pinned to it was an envelope with the words *Read me* printed on it.

I opened the envelope and a gold cross attached to a chain fell out.

As he picked it up, Kyle whispered, "It's Emma's."

Mom had gotten it for her for Confirmation last year. Emma wore it all the time.

Also inside the envelope was a folded sheet of paper. I opened it and held it up so we could both read it: *Make Kyle wear the vest.*

"Like you could *make* me do anything," Kyle said with a smirk. Then he realized what he'd just said and his eyes widened. "Max, that's your handwriting!"

I nodded, speechless, wondering what it meant. I mean, obviously it meant that in some future, the future that I had come back from to leave this, Kyle was going to get shot. By the kidnapper? Or someone else?

I turned the paper over and looked inside the envelope. Nothing. Why didn't I give more information?

"We make it home," Kyle began, "or at least you do and maybe Emma, too, and you're able to come back again and leave us a clue, and *this* is the lame clue you leave?"

I did not tell him I'd been thinking the same thing. "It'll probably save your life."

After a moment he put on the vest.

"How did you get this?" I asked Samuel, when he climbed out of the tree.

He crouched, picked up a stick, and began spreading the ashes from his cold campfire. Then he tossed on a couple logs and some kindling and sat back. "I found it here yesterday when I got back from a hunt. Why would you leave that here?"

"It means that we makes it back," Petra put in. "Or at least Max does. With Emma."

It didn't, really, but it did make it more likely.

"Why would anyone take Emma in the first place?" Kyle asked.

I still didn't have a good theory.

"Maybe someone's trying to get back at Mad Jack Pierson," I said.

"By kidnapping his great-great-great-granddaughter?" Kyle asked.

He had added one too many *greats*, but I didn't comment on that.

I shrugged. "I didn't say it made sense."

"Do you think someone's trying to change the past?" Petra wanted to know. "Isn't that the plot of every *Star Trek* time-travel episode?"

I gave her a look. I would never have guessed that she watched *Star Trek*.

"Usually," I said, "the bad guys try to change the present or future by changing the past." And then the Starfleet people have to go back and try to fix things. Except in the reboot movie where they killed like nine billion Vulcans, and no one seemed to care. "How do you think Emma could be involved?"

Kyle wasn't listening. "You think someone came from the future to grab her? Does that mean that we're not where we're supposed to be?"

"No," I said, "because they're changing our present in the past so their future is also changed. In their present. But they could've also come from the past."

He snorted. "I have no idea what you just said." Then he gestured. "And why is Samuel here?"

No one answered.

We decided to make camp there that night—Samuel had said that his cave was less than a day's walk from the stump and that there was a large lake not far from there, which was probably where the launch was going.

The four of us sat in a kind of semicircle around the fire and made dinner with the last of the granola bars. They didn't go far and we were all a little hungry at the end of the meal, but Samuel said there was a place we'd be able to do some hunting or gathering tomorrow.

After we'd eaten, Petra tossed Aki small chunks of her ration—a peanut butter granola bar. The dromaeosaur chick used both his mouth and front claws to pluck pieces off. Every now and then, he would pounce and slash with his back legs.

The lab books were still in my backpack, because I didn't want Samuel to know about them yet. They probably needed more drying out, anyway. Assuming they hadn't liquefied by now.

Kyle wore the bulletproof vest over his T-shirt, which still sort of surprised me. He had to have been pretty hot, but now that I thought about it, probably no worse off than in football pads in August. He was still moving stiffly from the bruises, but hadn't complained. My ankle was throbbing a little too, but I didn't mention that, either.

As we relaxed after our meal, Petra asked, "Samuel, what's life like in 1919?"

Sitting cross-legged next to her, he was quiet for a moment. "It's home. My father is a university professor. He's thinking we might move to Hyde Park, near the streetcar line." Samuel gestured across the fire at Kyle and me. "I suppose to y'all, that's ancient stuff. So what's the twenty-first century like?"

Petra began, "Well, for one thing—"

"Wait." Sitting up, I startled Aki. "Don't answer that."

"Why not?" Petra replied, as she held out a hand to soothe the hatchling dinosaur.

I looked over first at Samuel, then at Kyle, before addressing Petra directly. "Because we don't know if he's telling the truth about how he got here, and we don't know what could happen if he finds out about the future."

"I've told y'all the truth," Samuel protested.

"Max is right," Kyle interjected. "Listen, I don't know if we can change the past, but we can't risk it. So we have to try not to tell Samuel anything that could affect—"

"But I wouldn't," Samuel interrupted.

"—even by accident."

Kyle was right, but I still had a nagging feeling we were being set up. And what was the "real" past, anyway?

After a moment Petra nodded from across the fire. "Something about that vest is bothering me."

"What about it?" I asked.

"Okay." She leaned forward. "Future-you left it because you knew current-you would be there, or Samuel would be there, or whatever, right?"

I nodded.

"That means that originally you didn't have the vest, right?" she asked. "Does that mean you can change the past? Or change the future by changing the past?"

"I don't know," I said. "Maybe. I guess."

"I think," Kyle put in, "that you have to be able to change things. That the past can't be fixed . . . because the Chronal Engine makes it possible to meet people in the past, and otherwise the people we meet in the past aren't people, they're, I don't know . . ."

I thought about that for a moment, trying to sort out the syntax. "But, then," I said, "do we have the right to change things . . . or even go to the past? I mean, to do things that could affect whether people in the future exist or not."

Even to save Emma. Except that she shouldn't have been here in the first place, either.

Samuel, who had remained silent throughout the conversation, now looked thoughtful. "If you did, you'd never be able to tell, so does it matter?"

"I don't know," I replied. But it sounded wrong.

"Right, then," Samuel said, but he had a look on his face that made me wonder what he was thinking.

< 109 >

NIGHT MOVES

THAT NIGHT, AT SAMUEL'S INSISTENCE, PETRA SLEPT IN THE hollowed-out tree trunk, while Kyle, Samuel, and I slept on the ground by the fire. (She seemed to think he was being chivalrous and not sexist.)

I woke up from a deep sleep once. For a moment I thought it was time for my watch, but then realized no one had tapped my shoulder.

Then I heard a soft noise of someone moving around. Probably, I figured, whoever was on watch, tending the fire. But something made me cautious. I moved my head slowly to peer over, so as not to draw attention.

Samuel was crouched on the other side of the fire, lit by the flickering flames. He was staring into a backpack beside him. My pack, I suddenly realized. The one with my laptop and the lab notebooks.

I sat still and watched, wondering what he was looking for.

Then he pulled out one of the notebooks and opened it.

"Hey!" I yelled, and sat up. "What are you doing?"

< 110 >

He looked over, startled, and I walked around the fire toward him, ignoring the twigs and rocks my bare feet were stepping on.

"Umm." He pushed the notebook back into the pack.

"What is it?" Petra asked as she peeked her head out of the tree.

"He was going through our backpacks," I said.

Samuel said nothing, while Kyle, sitting up, gave me a long look.

"You weren't dreaming?" Kyle asked.

"Oh, come on," I replied. "I was not dreaming." Just because once, when I was eight, I'd been convinced that someone had broken into the house next door, and, well, let's just say the police were called and Mr. Mims wasn't too mad, although he did move to Florida not long afterward.

"Just checking," Kyle said. "All right, Samuel, what's going on?"

"I knew we shouldn't trust him!" I put in.

"Trust *me*?" Samuel said. "I'm the one who shouldn't trust you! I'm not the one with the, the whatever you called it, Recall Device! I just happened to appear here out of nowhere! How do you think y'all look to me?"

"Why were you going through my backpack?" I asked.

He hesitated. "I wanted to see what you were hiding . . . if anything. How did you get those books?"

"Never mind that!" I exclaimed. "You can't—"

"Max, shut up!" Kyle said, glaring at me. "Samuel, can you read any of those?"

< 111 >

"Are you kidding me?" I told my brother. "How can we trust him if—"

"We don't have a choice," Kyle answered. "We're the only ones here, and our number-one priority is rescuing Emma and getting home. Nothing else matters."

"How do we know he isn't in on it with the kidnapper?" I demanded.

"Why would he be?" Petra asked, still in the tree trunk. "He's already got Emma. The kidnapper, I mean. There's no reason to send a spy."

Kyle nodded.

"I did not kidnap your sister," Samuel said.

"What's in *your* backpack?" I asked, not ready to let it go.

He reached for his pack and upended it, dumping its contents on the ground near the fire. "Satisfied?"

I stepped over and prodded the pile with my foot. Clothes, toiletries, first-aid kit. Nothing remarkable.

In the distance something screeched, startling us all.

"Listen." Samuel glanced back into the forest. "We're stuck here together . . . I'm sorry. If we're all to survive and get back home, we have to work together."

He held out his hand.

I hesitated, considering. He could've been lying. He could've been telling the truth. But it was late. There was no way everything would get resolved right then, anyway. And he may have been right, at least on the part about working together to get home.

We shook on it. *"Were* you able to read anything in the notebooks?"

"No."

I awoke disoriented, wondering what had possessed me to camp out, and my back was sore from the ground. Then I remembered where I was. When I was.

Standing, I saw that Petra was still asleep, Aki curled in the crook of her arm.

After the incident with the backpacks, I'd been more than happy to stay awake and take over from Samuel. The night watch had been uneventful. After killing about a thousand mosquitoes and trying not to worry too much about the hair-raising screeches deep in the forest, I'd handed off to Kyle.

I stretched. The morning wasn't as hot as the day, but it would never be cool. Maybe about eighty. And humid.

Samuel was asleep, too, lying beside his backpack, bow and quiver up against the tree trunk.

I glanced toward the riverbank, where Kyle sat, legs crossed, on a rock next to a cypress. For a moment I was anxious, but the bank here was too high for a gator to climb. Beside him lay a branch that had been trimmed into a spear.

As I approached, I began, "Hey—"

Kyle shushed me and pointed just upriver, at a bend, where another cypress rose from the bank. An *Ornithomimus* stood, peering into the shadows between the tree and the bank. About six feet tall, it looked sort of like a slim, less feathery ostrich, but with a long tail and arms, not wings, that ended in claws.

It stood still a moment, head cocked, until with a quick darting movement, its head and neck struck at something on the ground.

When it came up, it was holding a lizard in its teeth. Another quick movement, and the lizard was swallowed whole.

I took a step forward, crunching a dried fern branch.

Startled by the noise, the *Ornithomimus* looked over at me, then turned and ran off through the ferns, upriver.

"Sorry," I whispered in response to Kyle's glare, and sat on the riverbank beside him. For a while we both listened to the water gurgling.

I stared into the river, watching as the currents flowed around a rock, swirling, sometimes bubbling, as leaves and bits of wood meandered downstream. Schools of fingerlings darted in and out of the shadows.

That reminded me. "What do you remember from Dad's funeral?"

Kyle turned his head slowly toward me. "What?"

It was something we never talked about. At least Kyle and Emma never talked about it with me.

"Do you remember anything about Grandpa being there?" I

For a while we both listened to the water gurgling.

clarified. "Did he say anything to you?" I'd been eight and didn't really remember much of the day, but I was hoping maybe Kyle might've.

He gave me a thin smile that was more of a grimace. "He said it was my job now to take care of y'all."

"I don't need you to take care of me," I said. "City boy."

He threw a rock into the water. "Grandpa didn't say a word about a time machine."

Chapter
XIII

SUNNY-SIDE UP

WE CONTINUED UPRIVER, RELYING ON SAMUEL'S CLAIM THAT there was a lake a little over a day's walk away that he thought might be the launch's destination. Supposedly, en route was the cave where we could make a base camp.

I still didn't think it was a good idea to trust him, but Petra and Kyle didn't seem onboard with my suspicions, and we were already heading in that direction, anyway. I just hoped we weren't being led into a trap.

By early afternoon I was sweaty, footsore, hungry again, and in a lousy mood. My ankle had scabbed over, but still hurt. The aspirin weren't doing a whole lot of good.

The lab books, which had been sealed up almost all night, were better, but still damp, some of the pages sticking together. I was beginning to wonder if they'd ever get completely dry in this humid environment.

By tonight I thought I'd be able to take a look at them. Hopefully the ink hadn't all washed away.

The redwood trees offered shade, but no relief from the heat.

My T-shirt was soaked through, and some insect was making an incredibly loud, high-pitched, sawing noise that somehow made me feel even hotter.

I took a swig from my canteen, then jogged to where Samuel and Kyle had paused to stand at the top of a small rise.

"How much farther?" I asked.

"Not much," Samuel said with a gesture. "But we've arrived at lunch."

As I reached the top of the rise, I looked and had to laugh.

Laid out before us, surrounding a pond that was about twice the size of an Olympic pool—amid cycads, ferns, and stands of magnolias—was a nesting colony of what I thought might be *Leptoceratops*, ridiculous-looking, tiny relatives of the three-horned, elephant-sized *Triceratops*.

The sheep of the Cretaceous, they were called. No more than six feet long from nose to tail and about waist high, the *Leptoceratops* didn't have horns, but they did have enormous heads with a bony frill and huge, parrot-like beaks. Their hind legs were much larger than their forelimbs, so they looked completely out of balance on all fours.

The effect was even more comical when they hoisted themselves up on their hind legs to run or "box" with each other.

Spread out in the shallow valley were almost a hundred nests, crater-like mounds about six feet in diameter and about ten feet apart. Most nests had at least one *Leptoceratops* near it, either lying down or adjusting the vegetation that at least partially covered the eggs.

"You said 'lunch'?" I asked, turning to Samuel.

"Eggs," Samuel replied. "I reckon if we were here awhile, we could come back and do some real hunting, but today I think we should just raid some nests and get to the cave as soon as possible. Especially with tyrannosaurs out and about."

I stared down at the colony. Most nests had a guardian. And even though they weren't big by dinosaur standards and looked cute and all, *Leptoceratops* were still big enough to be dangerous.

"Look over there," I said. Ahead and to my right, a couple of the *Leptoceratops* were rooting around at the base of a cycad. "That's what the beaks are for. If they can cut through a cycad trunk, they can do the same to an ankle. Or an arm. And they're going to be protecting those nests."

Samuel leaned on his bow. "We have fire."

"You want to burn them out?" I said, my tone kind of hostile. I pictured a stampede and a field full of charred eggs.

"We just need a few torches," Samuel explained. "We drive them back and take the eggs." He pulled out his bowie knife and approached a tree.

The bark seemed to be peeling slightly. Samuel plunged the knife into the trunk, then drew it downward. Before long, he had a sheet of bark, which he rolled into a narrow cone. "Birch-bark torches."

< 119 >

"Oh, give me a break!" Petra said. "We also have these." She raised her bow, Aki still on her shoulder. She pointed a bit to the left of straight ahead. "There."

Then she nocked an arrow to the string, aimed, and shot, before anyone could say anything. The broad-head struck the *Leptoceratops* she was aiming at (at least I assumed it was the one she was aiming at)—an animal with a nest at the edge of the herd. It made a noise somewhat like a combination of a pig's squeal and a sheep's bleat, and then fell over, but kept making the noise. Others of the herd around it made snorting noises and trotted a couple paces off. Then they stopped, not wanting, I guess, to leave their nests.

"Gentlemen," Petra said, "I give you an unprotected nest."

Leaning on his spear, Kyle hid a smile while Samuel looked outraged.

"We didn't need to do that!" Samuel said, dropping his birch-bark cone. "We can't take any of the meat with us. You wasted it!"

"Better the *Leptoceratops* than one of us," Petra replied. "This is survival, not camping. Besides, it isn't wasted. Something will come and eat it."

"Speaking of which," I said, "let's get some eggs before the something gets here."

I led the way down the hill into the valley, toward the colony, surveying the nesting dinosaurs and being eyed warily in return. Up close, the *Leptoceratops* looked less like Mesozoic comic relief and more like unpredictable wild animals.

"Nice fella," Kyle said in a soothing tone to the wounded *Leptoceratops* as we approached its nest. "Nice pig-dinosaur thing. We don't want to hurt you. We just want to kill you and eat your young."

I filled a pack with eggs while Kyle stood ready with his makeshift spear. In the meantime, Petra slit the *Leptoceratops*'s throat and pulled out her arrow.

"You sure we can't bring any of this with us?" Petra asked.

"Not with tyrannosaurs running around," Samuel replied, a little stiffly. "We need to get out of here and get the blood cleaned off you. Posthaste."

I hoisted the egg bag and turned to go.

"Umm, guys," I said. Our path back was cut off by a pair of *Leptoceratops*. They didn't look like they'd really even noticed us, but they were in the way. I took a step, figuring I'd just skirt behind the one on the left, which it must've seen, because it gave an angry bleat and stood facing me, raising its frill to make it look bigger.

The *Leptoceratops* took a two-step warning charge at me, but then stopped.

"Oh, this is ridiculous," Petra said, raising her bow again.

"No!" Samuel yelled, as the *Leptoceratops* let out a shrill trumpet, then charged.

Kyle stepped forward, lowered his spear, and thrust it at the creature's face. The spear struck the top of the bony frill and glanced away.

Then, lunging forward, the *Leptoceratops* knocked Kyle into
Samuel, who tried to dodge back.

With another bleat, the *Leptoceratops* shook its head, brushing off the blow.

Then, lunging forward, the *Leptoceratops* knocked Kyle into Samuel, who tried to dodge back.

"Watch out!" Kyle yelled as he and Samuel hit the ground.

The *Leptoceratops* ignored them and continued forward into the colony.

But Petra and I were blocking the creature's path.

As I lowered my quarterstaff, the animal caught it with its beak.

With a snap of its jaws, the *Leptoceratops* cut the staff in two and grunted twice, pawing the ground.

Then Petra jabbed at the animal with the bloody arrow she'd taken from her kill.

The *Leptoceratops* paused, flanks heaving, as it let out a bellow.

Meanwhile, Kyle and Samuel got untangled and edged out of the way, clear of the colony's stragglers.

A moment later the *Leptoceratops* grunted once more, then trundled off to the side, ignoring us completely.

We retreated from the nesting ground, up the gentle incline to our overlook spot on the rise. Petra washed her hands with water from her canteen.

Taking a glance back, I saw the *Leptoceratops* whose nest we'd raided lying stiff on the ground. I felt a brief moment of regret, but to be honest, I couldn't tell whether it was because we'd killed the creature or because we weren't taking any of its flesh.

I wondered what the eggs would taste like. And how Emma was faring.

And then I heard a loud squealing. When I found the source, I saw a *Nanotyrannus* on the other side of the colony approach the herd. Another came out of a stand of cycads immediately behind.

The nearby *Leptoceratops* shied away, parting like a sea.

The pair eyed the herd, trying to select, I guess, one to go after.

Then they must've picked up the scent of the dead animal, because they lowered their heads, looking in our direction.

Petra fitted an arrow to her bow. "Why don't we get out of here?"

"Wait," Samuel said, although he, too, nocked an arrow.

"What for?" I asked as the *Nanotyrannus* came closer.

"To make sure they're stopping," Samuel said. Even as he spoke, the *Nanotyrannus* pair walked up to the *Leptoceratops* and, from either side, began to devour it.

The same pair I had seen two nights ago.

"Now we should go," Samuel announced.

"I don't understand it," Petra said, as we grabbed our packs and Aki and left.

"What?" I asked when no one else did.

"How do . . . how do these sheep things survive?" she asked. "I mean, they have these nests on the ground out in the open, and they're totally defenseless. *Anything* can come and eat them or steal their eggs."

"Yeah," Kyle said. "It's like Luby's cafeteria only it's all free, and you don't need a tray."

"Yes." Petra shook her head. "It's exactly like Luby's."

"They survive," I said, "the same way animals like ostriches, alligators, and turtles survive. They lay a lot of eggs, so there's a good chance at least some of them will make it. Plus, there are a lot of them here, which means that any given predator is only going to get one. Most will survive."

"And I don't know how defenseless they are," Kyle added. "They did a number on Max's quarterstaff."

It wasn't long before we had left the colony far behind.

Every now and then, I would pause, listening to make sure we weren't being followed by the two *Nanotyrannus*.

BAD DINOSAUR

WE HIKED THE REST OF THE AFTERNOON WITHOUT TAKING A break, angling back along the low ridge overlooking the river. It was hotter now, and we were all moving more slowly than before.

Then the trees opened up, and Samuel stopped. "Well, what do you think?"

We were on an outcrop about seven or eight feet up, the river to our left and a creek cutting through an arroyo in front of us. The ground was rockier here, fewer ferns and only a couple sickly-looking cycads.

"I think," Kyle said, looking to the opposite side of the arroyo, "these are nice rocks."

The arroyo wall on the far side of the creek was about fifteen feet high. Set into it, almost directly across from us, was a cave about halfway up. An obviously hand-built ladder led from the creek bed to a narrow terrace in front of the cave mouth, and another from the terrace up to the top of the arroyo cliff. They were made from branches and lashed together with what looked like vines.

From the cave mouth, you'd have a view of both the river and the creek on the other side. From where we stood, I could see the creek splash down to a waterfall and a small clear pool, before cascading down another waterfall to make its way to the river about a hundred feet beyond.

On the other side of the creek, beyond the cave, rose a steep, rocky hill, covered with ferns and cycads, as well as a smattering of fir trees.

"You built those?" Petra asked, peering at the ladders.

"With a rock and a bowie knife," Samuel answered.

"Come on," Kyle said to me as we climbed down into the arroyo. "You still have the binoculars?"

"Yeah, why?"

Without waiting for an answer, he crossed the water and ran up the ladder to the cave ledge. Despite his bruised side, he was out of sight, over the top of the second ladder before I made it to the cave mouth.

"Hey, wait!" I yelled, dropping my backpack on the ledge. "You don't know what's up there!"

It took me a few seconds to open my pack and find the binoculars, so even wearing his own pack and holding his spear, Kyle was about a quarter of the way up the hill by the time I'd made it to the top of the arroyo, crossed to the base of the hill, and started climbing after him.

"Stay here!" I told Petra and Samuel, who had followed me to the top of the arroyo.

"Last one up has to do the dishes," Kyle called down.

"Wait!" I yelled again. "Slow down!"

He ignored me, reaching the summit long before me.

"Just like when coach makes us do stadium stairs back home," he said, when I finally joined him.

"Huh," I replied, breathing heavily. "And here I thought you were just trying to impress Petra."

He grunted, and we looked around in a circle at the top of the hill.

To the west, the sun was setting. Down below, we could see the river snake its way through the hills. Across the river, a gently hilly flatland was covered with ferns and stands of conifers and then rose to a cluster of smaller hills. On our side, the land was contoured, like the Texas Hill Country, but eventually leveled out into a more open expanse.

We could see herds moving below, on the other side. *Triceratops*, probably, and some kind of crestless hadrosaur. Smaller herds or packs, maybe, of two-legged ornithopods grazed and darted nearby.

Farther up was a swampy-looking lake, with cypresses and lily pads growing out of the water. And on a spur of land sticking into the lake, on the near side, was a charming little quaint wooden cottage and some kind of work shed a little distance beyond.

"That's it!"

We high-fived, and then Kyle pumped his fists in the air.

While he was celebrating, I took one more look out and around. A trio of pterosaurs was circling overhead. Samuel and Petra were standing near the edge of the arroyo, just above the cave, looking up at us. I waved.

Then I grinned and plunged down the hill. "Last one to the cave does the dishes!"

I had a good head start and I'd surprised Kyle, but I heard him make an exasperated noise and then start running.

A quick glance showed him gaining, with the spear held out away from him.

I almost made a joke about running with sharp objects, but I needed to concentrate on keeping my footing on the uneven ground.

Ahead, Petra and Samuel were still watching from the rocky ground near the ladder that led down to the cave.

I had just about reached them, dodging a cycad tree, when I felt a pair of hands shove into me from behind.

I went flying, and Petra shouted, "Look out!"

I struck the ground on my hands and knees, and my momentum carried me into Petra, slamming me into her below the knee. She immediately hit the ground next to me.

"Kyle!" I yelled, baffled and angry, and turned over, hands and knees stinging.

I didn't have time to say anything more.

A *Nanotyrannus* was looming over my brother. Kyle was down

on the ground, scrambling after his spear, right at the edge of the embankment.

He must've knocked me out of the way of its initial lunge.

And then the *Nanotyrannus* had Kyle's arm and shoulder gripped in its mouth.

An arrow struck it in the neck. Samuel stood off to the side, grimly nocking another arrow to his bowstring.

But the *Nanotyrannus* was still focused on Kyle, releasing its initial grip and grabbing him again so that Kyle's torso and left arm were in its mouth. As it lifted him up, another arrow struck its flank. And then another.

I ran forward, picked up Kyle's spear, and jabbed the *Nanotyrannus* in the side.

Finally, it released my brother, dropping him to the ground. It whirled on me, but slipped. Its claws scrabbled at the rocky ground, and it went down over the edge of the cliff.

I rushed over to where Kyle had been dropped face-down, shirt torn. His breath came in shallow rasps, his face pale.

But the vest had held. The *Nanotyrannus*'s teeth hadn't broken through. At least not to the chest. Kyle's arm looked bruised and bloody, though. And his backpack was completely mangled.

But that didn't explain how he was breathing.

"What's wrong?" I asked.

"Ribs," was Kyle's whispered reply.

And then I understood: the vest had protected Kyle from the teeth, but not the force of the jaws snapping shut. Broken ribs.

I tore off my shirt, using it to stanch the blood from his arm.

"You realize," I told him, "that was a totally illegal block."

He coughed in what might have been an attempt to hold back a laugh. Then he tried to look past me. "Where's Petra?"

ERRAND OF MERCY

"I'M OKAY," Petra said, but her voice was shaky. She sat on the ground, clutching her ankle. The one I'd knocked into. "But I think it's broken."

"Sorry," I whispered.

"Might be just a sprain," Samuel said. He'd come forward quietly, holding on to his bow. "Can y'all make it down the ladder?"

I glanced over the side of the arroyo embankment. On the creek bed, the *Nanotyrannus*—perforated and bleeding—was trying to climb to its feet. Part of me was astonished that the creature was still in any way mobile. But most tyrannosaur fossils showed evidence of severe injuries, so they were apparently built to take it. I didn't think this one would last long, though.

Petra stood, leaning heavily on Samuel. Together, they limped over to the ladder.

"Let me go first," he said, "so if you fall, I can catch you."

Petra snorted, leaning on one of the upraised legs of the ladder, but let him go.

Moments later she was over the edge and down the ladder to the cave terrace.

Looking down, I watched her hobble over to sit, back against the cliff. At the same time, Aki scurried out of the cave to cuddle in her lap. I hadn't realized until then he'd been down there.

Turning away from the edge, I asked Kyle, "Can you make it?"

He gritted his teeth, but nodded. I helped him up, then over to the ladder. His breathing was ragged as he slowly maneuvered down to the cave ledge.

Once on solid ground, he swayed, then collapsed to the ground next to Petra. I leaned him up against the cave wall and handed him his canteen.

Petra was staring down at the *Nanotyrannus*, which was limping upriver in the arroyo. "You know, that would've killed a mammal."

"Its friend will probably finish it off," Samuel said.

I pulled on an extra shirt and grabbed our first-aid kit from my pack.

Kyle sat stiffly, leaning against the side of the cave. He was pale, and his face was sweaty.

I cleaned the bite wound and bandaged his arm. It wasn't that deep, but there were a lot of teeth marks and he needed stitches. His backpack had taken most of the bite, I thought, or even the vest wouldn't have helped much. I showed him the tears and holes, lifting an eyebrow at his expression. He was breathing easier now, though.

Petra had removed her shoe and sock. Her ankle was swollen

and already bruising, but I didn't see anything like bone showing through the skin.

I handed them both some aspirin from the first-aid kit. Samuel wrapped Petra's ankle tightly in bandages he'd pulled from his own pack.

Then he gestured at Kyle. "You, too. It's all you can do for ribs. At least you're not coughing up blood. You didn't puncture a lung."

"We don't know they're broken," I said.

"Yes, we do," Kyle replied. "I've had bruised ribs before."

And Mom had had a fit.

"We need to get Kyle and Petra to a hospital," I told Samuel.

"We need one of your Recall Devices, then," he replied.

I was silent a moment. "And Emma."

Samuel and I could do it. Go after my sister. Kyle and Petra would have shelter from the cave and access to fresh water. They could also build a fire, although we were high enough up the arroyo wall that they'd be safe from predators, and it was warm enough they wouldn't need heat at night.

"Oh, no," Kyle said, shaking his head, wincing as Samuel wrapped the bandages around his torso. "You are not going—"

"We'll leave you the food and the majority of the supplies and Petra's bow," I interrupted. It was the only way. Samuel nodded. "And Samuel and I will go, and—"

"No!" Kyle said. He gestured. "You trust him now?"

"Do we have a choice?" I asked.

"You and Petra are in no shape to travel," Samuel added.

Kyle tried to stand, gritting his teeth and shaking with the effort. Then he reached out to grab the cave wall, sinking back down.

"Let them go," Petra said. She shook her head, then blinked. "We came for Emma, and at this point we'd be slowing them down." She coughed. "She's the only important one here."

"What?" I exclaimed.

"If we were the important ones, we'd have been taken. We have to get Emma back." Petra gave Kyle a long stare. "I don't think she can afford to wait much longer."

Finally, my brother groaned and swore. "First thing in the morning."

By now the sun had set, and the forest was becoming alive again with the sounds of night creatures.

"In the morning," Kyle insisted again.

He was right. We couldn't go now. Even with the nearly full moon, the forest was too dark, the shadows big enough to hide a *Nanotyrannus*, and we'd already seen two of them out at night. Which meant that their bigger cousins might occasionally be active at night, too.

But whether that kind of thing was isolated or regular behavior, no one knew, and I didn't really want to find out. Or maybe I did. But in a safe, non-disemboweled way.

< 135 >

I was lying on my back, hands behind my head, inside the cave. For the first time since we'd gotten there, that night I couldn't sleep, and not just because my knees and hands and the cut on my ankle were hurting. It wasn't that I was hungry, either. I was full from the *Leptoceratops* embryos—turns out they tasted sort of like frog legs.

Although the cave entrance was small, Samuel's refuge opened up beyond, going back about fifteen feet. It was almost as wide, shaped like an irregular oval. Kyle was lying on a pile of fir branches Samuel had made into a mattress, snoring. He slept fitfully, feverish, muttering, and, every now and then, thrashing his good arm.

Petra also slept, but sitting up, legs extended, leaning against the cave wall. Aki lay curled in her lap. Samuel was outside, crouched by the fire on the cave terrace.

I got up, stepped over Petra's legs, and went out and sat cross-legged, looking down at the creek.

A moment later Samuel joined me, holding two tin cups with little conifer branches sticking out. He handed me one. "Fir tea. It has vitamin C. Prevents scurvy."

I sipped. It tasted terrible.

For a while we sat in silence, listening to the sound of the waterfall and some strange barking and hooting noises that were coming from the direction of the river. Moonlight shone onto the cave ledge, but the forest on the other side was dark.

I was thinking about my brother and sister. It had always been them. The twins. Sticking up for each other. Getting each other in trouble. Getting each other out of trouble. This was the longest they'd been apart that I could remember.

I'd never seen anyone as beat up as Kyle before. Broken ribs were one thing. But he could also have internal injuries and bleeding. Those could kill him.

Then there was the bite. It wasn't that deep and the bleeding had almost stopped, but tyrannosaur bites were thought to be infectious, and we didn't have any high-power antibiotics. Which could also mean death.

And Petra. Sure, she only had a broken ankle. But you could die from a broken bone, too, I thought. At least that's what happened in that book Emma had to read for honors English last year about some jerk who pushed his best friend out of a tree.

And who knew what condition Emma was in? She could be even worse off.

As long as I could walk, Kyle would never forgive me if I let anything happen to her.

It was up to me now.

"We have to go," I said, putting down the tea.

"I was wondering when that would occur to you," Samuel murmured.

We would travel light.

I took my backpack and only some of the supplies. We left Kyle

< 137 >

and Petra all but one of the canteens and almost everything else, except a flashlight and Samuel's bow. We decided we'd leave the lab books and laptop computer, as well as the nonfunctioning Re-call Device. In case we didn't make it, they might have a second, desperate chance.

"We ready?" Samuel asked.

I nodded.

"Try not to do anything dumb," Kyle said, his voice rasping.

I guess we hadn't been as quiet as I'd thought. "Thanks."

And we were off.

DOGTROT

THERE WAS MORE LIGHT THAN I'D EXPECTED. ONCE WE WERE heading in the right direction, away from the creek, the moon was bright. It was nearly full, and the sky was clear. More clear than I'd ever seen it.

If we stayed in the open, we almost didn't need to use the flashlight.

What I expected to see, more than dinosaurs even, were mammals. Multituberculates, like the ones we'd seen the other day (was it really only yesterday?), or maybe marsupials. Possums.

"You don't trust me," Samuel said in an amused tone, after we'd walked for a while.

"Like I said, I don't have a choice anymore." He *had* saved Kyle with his shooting and probably Petra and me, as well. But there was still something a little off about him. We walked a bit longer and then I decided not to hold back. I stopped and looked him in the eye. "I think you've been here longer than ten days and that you know more about Mad Jack Pierson than you're saying. Why don't you just tell us?"

"Well, now." Samuel took a swig from the canteen, then handed

CHRONAL ENGINE

it to me. "Look at it from my perspective. I'd been camping with my brother, and then all of a sudden I'm here. In the very, very antediluvian past. Alone, like Robinson Crusoe. At least y'all came here on purpose. I'd never heard of this Mad Jack Pierson until y'all mentioned him.

"Maybe, though," Samuel went on, "you don't trust me, not because I'm not trustworthy, but because you're the suspicious type." He took another swig. "That's not necessarily a bad thing. I'm just saying . . ."

Still scanning the moonlit forest ahead, I opened my mouth to reply, but then broke off with a slight gasp.

"What is it?"

"Over there." I pointed. Ahead and to the right. At the edge of the forest.

A mound. Sort of like the *Leptoceratops* nests, but bigger and completely covered by a dome of vegetation. Next to it, lying asleep between a pair of dawn redwoods, was a tyrannosaur.

Not one of the cute, little tiny ones like the *Nanotyrannus* that had nearly killed my brother. This one was full-grown or at least close to it. Thirty, maybe forty feet long, with a mouth that could swallow you whole. It looked even bigger than the one we'd seen when we first arrived in the Beetle.

Samuel froze. "How many do you see?"

"One," I answered. "Why? How many do *you* see?"

He shook his head. "Then, let's go this way."

< 140 >

He whirled and backtracked a couple minutes before heading back upriver in a wide arc around the sleeping giant.

"I suppose that mound was a nest?" Samuel said once we were clear.

"Probably," I replied. I don't think paleontologists have discovered a real tyrannosaur nest yet, though.

He didn't say anything more for a while. "When we come back, why don't we try a different route?"

By the time we reached the lake, just at dawn, I was practically sleepwalking. I was briefly jealous of Aki and Kyle and Petra back in the cave. Then I decided that, no, I wouldn't really rather have a sprained ankle or broken ribs, and that leftover *Leptoceratops* eggs were probably completely gross.

The lake was still. Cypresses grew into the water, while redwoods stood tall in the distance, on the other side. At the near shore, giant lily pads grew and frogs croaked. A few hundred yards to our right, about a dozen crestless hadrosaurs waded in the shallows.

"Oh, this is bad," I said. We emerged from a stand of magnolias to see the cottage a couple hundred yards off. Unfortunately, about a hundred yards of that was a channel.

The cottage was on an island.

Kyle and I hadn't seen that when we'd been up on the hill.

"Can you swim?" Samuel asked.

"Yes."

"Can Emma?"

"State champion individual medley in her age group." I wasn't sure I wanted to swim, though. I didn't think the *Deinosuchus* would be here in the lake, but there could be other dangerous things. Freshwater sharks, for example.

"The launch isn't here," Samuel said.

I took a closer look. It wasn't at the dock, and I didn't see it anywhere on the lake. "Downriver, then." I looked through the binoculars at the house.

The building itself was a standard Texas dogtrot, two cottages with the dogtrot breezeway between them, and a single roof. There had been a lot of them in Texas in the nineteenth and early twentieth centuries, and it made sense here: the breezeway provided shade and drew in air from the outside. At least that was the theory.

This dogtrot had a wooden pier extending from a wooden walkway behind it. Each side of the cottage had a pair of windows.

Off to the rear, about ten or so yards away, was a small blocky building and what looked like a gas tank. A generator, probably. Whoever had built this place made sure it had all the twentieth-century amenities.

There were no signs of humanity. That could mean that Emma was on the boat, or it could mean she was locked in one of the rooms.

Then there was a screech, and Samuel exclaimed, "Giant rocs!"

I lowered the binoculars to look. About a half dozen pterosaurs were landing at the water's edge. Folding their wing membranes up to walk on all fours, they began wading into the lake in front of us.

"*Quetzalcoatlus*," I said. There was a skeleton of one at the Texas Memorial Museum.

"Named for the Aztec serpent god?"

I nodded. They had a thirty-five-foot wingspan, give or take. They were thought to be able to eat fish and small animals. Of course, to them, we were "small animals."

There were seven of them now, wading, peering down into the water. They stood upright, not sprawling, eleven, maybe fifteen feet tall. Like giraffes, but with six-foot beaks and leathery wing membranes that connected their front legs and back.

And they were between us and the island.

"What now?" Samuel asked.

The *Quetzalcoatlus* closest to us plunged its head into the water, snapping its mouth shut. When it pulled it up, a giant fish wriggled, struggling to get free. The pterosaur tossed its head and swallowed the prey whole.

"I think," I said, "we run for it. The water looks pretty shallow." It was hard to tell exactly, considering how big the pterosaurs were, but it didn't look like the water was more than a few feet deep. We might be able to make it to the cottage without having to swim.

Samuel nocked an arrow to his bowstring, then nodded at me.

< 143 >

We left the cover of the woods, making our way past the rushes to the lakeshore.

The *Quetzalcoatlus* ignored us, intent on their fishing.

We waded into the murky water. When we were almost up to our knees and about a quarter of the way to the dock, something brushed past my calf. "What was that?"

"Fish. Probably spawning," Samuel answered, but he was looking from side to side at the pterosaurs. The two largest were to our left. "How fast are these giant roc things?"

"Paleontologists really aren't sure," I said, still trying to figure out what was in the water. "Some people think they were really awkward on land and not good at wading, either. In fact, the idea that they could exhibit terrestrial predation is considered controversial. Historically, they've been thought of as surface skimmers, feeding on fish."

"Thank you, Professor."

I glanced in the direction Samuel was aiming an arrow. One of the *Quetzalcoatlus* on the left had noticed us. It took a couple steps, splashing the shallow water toward us.

"You should run. Now." Samuel released the arrow and then took off for the island before waiting to see if he'd hit his target. I ran beside him, splashing, the water slowing us both.

We were about three-quarters of the way to the dock when we lost our footing and pitched forward. We'd reached a drop-off of maybe four feet.

< 144 >

"You should run. Now." Samuel released the arrow and then took off
for the island before waiting to see if he'd hit his target.

As I kicked forward into a swim, I saw the *Quetzalcoatlus* was nearly on top of us.

"Dive!" I shouted. I plunged beneath the water's surface and began frog swimming. I felt a shock wave as the *Quetzalcoatlus's* snout struck deep. And then another. And then it was gone. My lungs burning, I swam a few more strokes and then surfaced and looked back.

The pterosaur had its back to me now as it stalked something underwater. Someone.

Then a surge of water caught me in the face. It was another of the *Quetzalcoatlus*, one of the group on the right, marching through the channel toward me.

But the dock was close.

I dived again, not coming up for air until I was underneath it and felt the ground sloping up to the island shore.

I turned to crouch next to one of the pilings only to see the *Quetzalcoatlus's* legs too close. Farther out in the channel, I saw the first pterosaur still trying to find Samuel. His hat floated free, between the creature's legs.

A jaw struck downward once, right next to the pier. I waited for the *Quetzalcoatlus* to decide it couldn't get to me, but it stayed, taking a step or two back and forth along the dock.

I had to get out from under. Samuel couldn't last much longer and who knew when the kidnapper would be back?

I slid to the end of the pier, banging my knee on a rock. From there, I was within a few feet of the *Quetzalcoatlus*'s foreleg.

It was big. But their bones were hollow. They had to be, so they could fly.

I reached down, clawing away mud and pebbles to release the rock I'd hit my knee on. It was about the size of a football.

Picking it up, I heaved it at the *Quetzalcoatlus*'s leg. It gave a squawk and splashed off.

Then I moved—half crawling, half walking—up the length of the dock, emerging finally on dry land.

A pile of split firewood was stacked onshore, an axe lying on the ground next to it. For the steamboat, probably. I grabbed an armful of the cut logs and ran out to the end of the pier. The first *Quetzalcoatlus* was still watching the surface of the water.

I shouted, then threw one of the split logs and then another. Both missed, but the splashes caught the pterosaur's attention. The third log hit it in the left rear leg. It stood a moment, staring at me. I yelled again and kept heaving the firewood. Several of the chunks of wood hit the creature in the wing membrane.

Finally, the *Quetzalcoatlus* moved off.

"Samuel!" I shouted, but didn't see him. Then I spotted a shape in the water, about twenty feet from the dock. I leaped off the pier back into the lake and swam out.

It was Samuel. Unconscious.

Half swimming, half walking along the bottom of the channel, I managed to drag him up into the horsetails that lined the shore of the island.

CPR, he needed CPR. All I knew about that was what I'd seen on TV. Emma, though. She'd taken the Red Cross course last year, even though she was technically too young.

"Emma!" I shouted, and ran toward the cottage, picking up the axe as I went. I entered the breezeway and paused at the four closed doors. "Emma!"

"Max?" came a voice from the far right door.

It was locked. "Stand back!"

After a couple blows of the axe, I shoved the door open. "Emma! No time! It's Samuel! He needs CPR!"

She blinked, but nodded. "Who's Samuel?"

"This way!" We raced out to where I had left him.

She rolled him over on his back, then shoved at his sternum. Water gushed from his nose and mouth. I climbed up on the dock while Emma performed CPR. The *Quetzalcoatlus* were down at the far end of the island, still hunting fish. I didn't think they'd be coming near again anytime soon.

After a moment I heard a cough, then another. I glanced down to see Samuel sitting up, Emma crouched beside him.

"You're . . . Emma?"

Emma was likewise frozen, staring open-mouthed. "Who are you?"

"This is Samuel," I said, climbing down beside her. "Samuel, this is my sister."

Emma stood and stepped back from him. I finally got a good look at her. Her clothes were dirty and she had a bruise on her cheek, but otherwise she looked healthy. I felt a rush of relief and swallowed, not trusting myself to speak.

Before I could say anything, she embraced me in a fierce hug. "I can't tell you how glad I am you're here. I've been locked up for a week and— Where's Kyle?"

I quickly filled her in on what had happened since she'd been taken. She didn't say anything, but drew in a quick breath when I told her about the *Nanotyrannus*.

"Okay," Emma said when I was through. She hugged me again. Then her voice was crisp. "Now, can one of you tell me why there's a picture of *this* guy in the workshop with Campbell?"

Samuel stepped forward, dripping. "I can explain."

"Who's Campbell? You mean the kidnapper?" I asked. "I *knew* there was something—"

"Come with me," Samuel interrupted, and rushed up into the breezeway.

Emma and I followed. Samuel picked up the axe from where I'd left it and hacked at the door across from Emma's. He forced it open and ran in, flicking a light switch. We entered behind him. The room was stuffy, but we ignored it. A ceiling fan began turning.

The room was a workshop—a machine shop. A thick wooden table stood on trestles along one wall. Mounted on it were a machine lathe and other equipment I didn't recognize. A bank of cabinets stood along another wall.

A framed black-and-white photo hung from a wall next to the door. It showed Campbell—the kidnapper—and a younger Samuel and an older man, Mad Jack Pierson. I recognized him from pictures in the basement back home.

"What's going on?" I asked.

Samuel was opening and closing little drawers in an apothecary cabinet. With a triumphant cry, he pulled out a small box and turned to us, a broad smile on his face. Our own expressions stopped him. Or maybe it was the fact that Emma was clutching the axe handle with both hands like she meant to use it. And not on a tree.

He swallowed. "I can use these to fix your Recall Device and get us home."

"What?" I demanded.

"Who *are* you?" Emma asked at the same time.

"And who's Campbell?" I put in.

Samuel was silent a moment, until Emma brandished the axe again.

"Isambard Campbell is my father's former assistant," he said, finally, "and failed graduate student."

"Your father . . ." I whispered, staring. "You're Mad Jack Pierson's *son?*" Which made Samuel Grandpa's *father?* My great-grandfather?

And he'd put us through all of *this?* "You son of—"

"Why did you and Campbell bring us here?" Emma interrupted. "And where's Pierson?"

"I don't know where my father is . . . and I had nothing to do with your being here," Samuel answered, holding up his hands. "I swear. That was all Campbell's doing."

"Why? What was he—"

"They had a falling out," Samuel said. "He and my father. Over the war, among other things. I think Campbell is trying to build his own Chronal Engine."

"Why?" I asked. "And what does it have to do with Emma?"

Samuel gave her another odd look. "Well, that's just the thing. She's the spitting image of the maidservant we had when I was younger, during the war, who my father always said was responsible for the breakthrough that led to the Chronal Engine. I always thought it was because Ella kept the place clean and organized, but now . . ."

"Ella?" I asked. "Emma's Ella?"

Emma lowered the axe. "Oh, this is just too weird."

"Why would Campbell have this picture up," I asked, "if he hates your father so much?"

"Because it's not his house," Samuel said. "It's my father's. The original house in Austin . . . he arranged to have it brought here when he moved to the ranch."

"Talk about getting away from it all," Emma muttered.

At that moment, from out on the lake, I heard a steam whistle.

And then multiple gunshots.

STALKED

"THAT'S CAMPBELL!" EMMA SAID.

"We've got to get out of here!" Samuel declared. He whirled around and pulled open a couple more cabinet drawers. Finally, he reached in and grabbed a package. Then he looked at Emma. "Is anyone else here? Any other prisoners?"

"No," Emma replied. "The other rooms are empty."

At that, we fled out into the breezeway, in the direction opposite the dock, and ran along the island shore, making sure we were out of sight of the dock. I didn't see the *Quetzalcoatlus*. They must've been scared away by the shots.

We dived into the water, wading and swimming across, until we reached the shore. Then we ran into the forest and under the cover of a pair of stubby palms.

We stopped to look, crouching in the undergrowth, as the launch glided up to the dock.

"That's my father's, too," Samuel muttered, as he pushed aside the top of a fern.

A man—Campbell—popped out of the cockpit and began tying the boat up.

"How did he get hold of it, then?" I blurted. "What did he do to your father? And why did he take Emma?"

Samuel hesitated. "I would guess that Ella—Emma—was bait. That my father disappeared or ran, and then Campbell brought Emma here to draw him out."

"Because without her, there's no Chronal Engine." I thought quickly. "At this point, he might as well still *have* Emma. He's got the only working Recall Device. We're stuck here."

"No, we're not," Samuel answered. "I told you, I can fix yours with these." He gestured with the packages he was holding, the ones he'd pulled out of the workshop.

"Which are what, exactly?" Emma put in.

"One's a watchmaker's tool kit," Samuel answered. "The other contains chronally resonant crystals."

"And what," I asked, with a glance at Emma, "is a 'chronally resonant crystal'?"

"It's hard to explain," Samuel said. "But if you apply an electric field in the right way, the crystals will resonate with a time signature that allows them to operate, to be tracked and modulated by the Chronal Engine." He shrugged. "The idea came to my father during a football game."

"In Dallas!" I exclaimed. "I know! I saw that in the notebook and—"

"Umm, guys, this is nice," Emma interrupted, "but shouldn't we

< 154 >

get moving?" Without waiting for an answer, she rose from her crouch and moved back from the tree line.

Over at the cottage, Campbell had finished tying up the boat, and was walking toward the dogtrot. In a moment, he'd find out Emma was gone.

I hurried after her, still questioning Samuel. "So there's one of these crystal things in the Recall Device, and it just *broke?*"

"Cutting them for both resonance and durability is a precise skill," he replied as we moved off. "If it's not done correctly, they become unstable. Most of the ones we have were made by Campbell. Rather shabbily."

We marched, occasionally looking back to see if Campbell was coming after us, and keeping an eye out for the fauna. The morning was alive with the calls of birds and the screams of other things too big to fly.

The meadows were almost overrun with dinosaurs. A group of *Triceratops* eyed us as we crossed through one. We made sure to keep our distance.

Once in a while, we'd come across a herd of small ornithopods that would bolt if we came too near.

We'd been walking for about an hour when we rounded a small grove of ginkgoes and came out straight at the edge of a pond, maybe a couple hundred yards wide and a hundred yards long. Ferns and horsetails grew at its edges.

"This wasn't here last night," I said.

Emma laughed, while Samuel shook his head.

"This way," he said, and led us along the edge of the pond, back toward, I assumed, the river.

We had just about cleared the south end of the pond when Samuel stopped abruptly. Ahead of us stood a full-sized tyrannosaur. Possibly the same one we'd seen last night, although I wasn't sure we were anywhere near the same area. The giant theropod was standing ankle deep in the marshy water, its back to us.

"Stand very still," Samuel said, holding up his hand. "We're downwind."

A moment later the tyrannosaur lumbered off into the forest.

At the next instant, there was a flash of light and a figure stepped from behind a cycad to our right.

It was Campbell. He was wearing khaki trousers and a crisp button-down shirt, with a blue bandanna around his neck. And he was carrying a revolver in one hand and a Recall Device in the other.

"Good morning, Samuel, Emma," he said. "And this must be Max."

The three of us didn't say anything.

"Now, Samuel," Campbell went on, "that's no way to treat an old family friend."

"Where's my father?" Samuel demanded.

< 156 >

"That's hardly germane." Campbell waved the gun. "What's important is that I have the gun and the Recall Device. And you have Emma and Pierson's lab notebooks. Which you will hand over to me now."

I didn't have them. I'd left them with Kyle and Petra. I shrugged my shoulders, though, letting my backpack fall. Then I hoisted it up and tossed it into the pond. "Run!"

Emma and I plunged through the ferny undergrowth, and a shot rang out behind us. We ran a few minutes, toward the river, I thought, and then stopped next to a redwood to see if we were being followed. "Where's Samuel?"

He burst out of the shrubbery. "Here! Come on!" Without waiting for us, he raced on, past a magnolia and into a sunnier, more open area. We followed and soon were right behind. Which was why we plowed into him when he suddenly stopped. He pitched forward over a mound of dead leaves and branches.

"What is it?" Emma asked. I looked back and could hear Campbell making his way through the plants, following.

"Nest!" Samuel said, as he scrambled to his feet.

He was right. It was a nest. A *big* nest. "And there's mama bear!"

The tyrannosaur stood about twenty-five yards to our right.

"Flank speed!" I shouted, and led the way off to our left. I ran as fast as I could, praying that adult tyrannosaurs really were as slow as some paleontologists thought.

I glanced back to see the creature standing there, maybe a step or two closer to the nest. Happy to drive us away from its young.

And then I ran into a barrier of cycads. More than six feet tall, the plants' sharp leaves sliced into my face and arms, and I tumbled to the ground.

Samuel and Emma pulled me to my feet, and, breathing heavily, we stared back at the tyrannosaur.

"We have to go around," I said. The cycads were too thick to plow through.

We were just heading around the grove when Campbell burst out of the woods on the other side to the clearing. He jumped atop the nest and fired his gun at us.

We froze.

"Idiot!" Samuel muttered.

"Look out!" I shouted, and pointed.

But he had already sensed or heard or saw or maybe smelled the danger. He whirled and, in a panic, began shooting at it.

It didn't faze the dinosaur at all. The tyrannosaur took two steps toward him and lunged. Then it grabbed Campbell in its mouth and lifted its head.

Emma screamed.

Campbell's legs, still visible, kicked out as he did what he should've done in the first place: activate the Recall Device.

The other side of the clearing was suddenly engulfed in a blinding flash and a cloud of smoke.

Campbell's legs, still visible, kicked out as he did what he should've done in the first place: activate the Recall Device.

A moment later we caught the smell of cooked meat.

When the smoke cleared, Campbell was gone. So was a portion of the nest. Part of a ginkgo tree. And the front half of the tyrannosaur. The rest, from about the waist back, lay crumpled on the ground, charred and smoking.

< 160 >

LAUNCHED

"IMAGINE THAT APPEARING SUDDENLY IN YOUR PARLOR," Samuel said.

At this Emma snickered, and we all burst into laughter.

"Seriously, though, what happened?" she asked. "Where's Campbell?"

"We think there are size limits," I said, remembering the diagram back at the Pierson ranch house, "on what the Recall Device can transport. It's why we couldn't bring the Hummer."

"There are," Samuel told us. "Mass limits, technically."

Emma took a swig of water from the canteen. "Great. Let's get home." She pointed. "Kyle and Petra are up this way?"

"Yes," Samuel answered, "but . . . Max, how far is the cave?"

"From here?" I shrugged. "Four, maybe five hours."

"And back to the cottage?"

"About an hour and a half."

"Then let's go there," Samuel said.

"How will that help?" We'd lose the time it would take to backtrack, and the boat wasn't that much faster than walking.

"Oh, didn't I mention it?" Samuel said with a thin smile. "There's

< 161 >

one built into the steamboat. It's how my father transported the materials for the cottage."

I stared a moment, angry again that he'd been holding out. Then it occurred to me. "Wait. Isn't the boat as big as a tyranno-saur? How did it not go up in smoke?"

"There are two versions of the Recall Device," Samuel answered. "The personal and the industrial." He grinned. "And, even fully loaded, the steamboat still has significantly less mass than a full-grown *T. rex*. But you should know that."

With another brief, self-satisfied grin, he headed back upriver.

Emma watched him go. "I'm not sure I like him—"

"Tell me about it," I replied.

We were there in a little over an hour. The boat was still tied up to the dock. The *Quetzalcoatlus* were gone.

At our approach a black bird took off from one of the pilings, and a pair of alvarezsaurs fled into the rushes.

The boat was identical to the one we'd seen wrecked, lying on the beach. Except this one was intact. I hoped that wasn't an omen for what was going to happen next.

The box—the industrial-strength Recall Device—we'd seen on the first boat, with the oxidized brass and copper, was 100 per-cent ready to go, Samuel announced.

We cast off, and he maneuvered us into the lake, away from shore.

He held up two fingers, set the control in the cockpit, and then we were gone, instantly reappearing downriver, at the mouth of the creek where Samuel's cave was.

"Over there." I dropped anchor, and then the three of us vaulted over the side of the launch onto a sandbar. We splashed our way up the creek to stand at the bottom of the ladder.

"Kyle! Petra!" Emma shouted. Without waiting for a reply, she began climbing.

Petra limped out onto the cave ledge and waved. A moment later Kyle was there too, moving stiffly, but with a broad smile on his face.

I got up to the ledge to see Emma embrace first Petra and then, more gently and with one arm, Kyle. With the other hand, she waved me in to the hug too.

"Good job, Baby Brother," Kyle said, holding out his fist to bump mine. "But you smell."

"Not as much as you," Emma said, as I returned the gesture. And the hug.

Long and short of it, in ten minutes and after a very hurried explanation, we were back aboard the boat with the remains of our supplies and a baby dromaeosaur.

"This thing's its own Recall Device, huh?" Kyle asked. At my nod he continued, "Why didn't you guys pop back here ten seconds after you'd left?"

With the other hand, she waved me in to the hug too.

"Because Campbell was in the boat on the river at the time," I said, "and it would've been very bad if we'd met him coming."

"Very bad," Emma said.

Samuel cleared his throat. "I did shave off a couple hours . . . Right now, Campbell will be arriving at the cottage."

This seemed to satisfy my brother.

"Everyone ready?" Samuel asked, and, without waiting for an answer, activated the Device.

We reappeared in our time, afloat on the Colorado River, in downtown Bastrop. Right next to the dock behind St. Joseph's Hospital, which I recognized because I needed stitches one time two years ago when we were staying at the resort just outside of town.

We'd made it home. Alive and mostly in one piece.

And in no time at all, really.

Only about an hour after we'd left.

As we tied up, Samuel suggested that he stay behind with the launch, both to protect the time machine and to ensure he didn't see too much of the future. Or so he said.

"No way," I told him. I was not going to leave him alone with the only working Recall Device. I was still wrapping my mind around the fact that he was our great-grandfather. And there was still a lot he hadn't told us.

In the end Emma agreed to stay with the boat and with Aki,

and Samuel helped me get our two injured up to the emergency room.

When we arrived at the glass window of the check-in desk, the nurse on duty stared at us in horror.

I knew what we must've looked like: damp with lake water and sweat, we hadn't had a hot shower in days, Petra was limping and had a cut on her head, and Kyle was beat up and bruised from the *Nanotyrannus* attack.

And Samuel looked like he'd just come out of an Indiana Jones movie.

"W-what happened to y'all?" the nurse stammered.

"Mauled by a bear," Kyle answered.

"Fell off a cliff," Petra said at the same time.

The nurse didn't look convinced, but called on an intercom, and a swarm of nurses and med techs came and wheeled Petra and Kyle away.

It took a lot of talking, but giving them my insurance card and telling them that Kyle was Rory Pierson's grandson and that Petra was Wilhelmina and Raul Castillo's daughter did wonders with the paperwork. The hardest thing was getting across that Grandpa was still in critical condition at the hospital in Austin and that Mom was out of reach in Outer Mongolia.

Finally, they stopped asking questions and told us to sit in the waiting area. A television playing baseball highlights hung above one corner, and a pile of magazines sat on a coffee table.

"*Now* you can leave," I told Samuel. He laughed, and we headed out of the emergency room. "But I want those extra crystals . . . and you have to tell me how to fit them into the Recall Device."

His grin was even broader than before. "I don't have to. The directions are in the lab books. The ones in English, anyway. The others are just nonsense."

"Wait, what do you mean?"

"My father made them out when he came to realize Campbell was trying to subvert his work," he explained. "They don't mean anything. The one in Japanese is just text copied from *Tale of Genji*, with some technical-looking pictures added. I think the French one is from *Les Misérables*. I don't know about the Hebrew. Probably from Genesis."

"But the notebooks are probably ruined," I said, "what with the water and dinosaurs and all."

Samuel shook his head. "Then just open the Device up. You'll be able to tell where the crystal goes."

We stopped at the riverbank. Emma was sitting back, relaxing on a bench in the sun.

"Don't knock yourself out," I said.

We climbed back onboard, and Samuel handed over the crystals.

I opened the box to make sure they were there. "So where does one find a chronally resonant crystal in the wild?"

"You can find a seam of the mineral just north of Fredericks-burg." Samuel climbed into the cockpit to check the control set-tings. "There's a gigantic Precambrian granite uplift that makes this mysterious sound that—"

"You mean Enchanted Rock?" I exclaimed. "It's what, like, four hundred feet high and covers a square mile!"

"The same," he said. "On the northwest side, not the whole rock." Then he looked serious. "Listen, I have to go find my father. I reckon he's probably back home having a drink at Sholz's Bier-garten but . . ." He gestured as if to tip his hat. "If y'all would like to come along . . ."

Despite my misgivings about Samuel, I was tempted, but wanted to make sure Kyle and Petra and Grandpa were okay.

"Look," I said. "I'm sorry I didn't . . ." My voice trailed off. I really wasn't sorry I hadn't trusted him. I still didn't. Not completely, anyway.

Not the way I trusted Kyle and Emma.

Samuel shook his head. "You probably shouldn't have." He hes-itated. "I did want to thank you for coming back for me in the channel. Both of you." He held out his fist. "Is this how it goes?"

"Yeah." We bumped.

We said our goodbyes and disembarked. I hoisted a pack with the lab books and Recall Device, while Aki watched the whole thing from Emma's shoulder.

Back ashore, while I tossed Samuel the lines, Emma stopped and called, "Wait. I still don't understand. How did you get there in the first place? And why?"

He gestured, looking genuinely sorry. "I'd tell you, but Max already told me it's bad to know too much about his future."

And then he and the launch vanished. With a flash of light and a booming sound.

"What did that mean?" Emma asked as we walked back up the manicured grass to the emergency room.

"It means," I said, "that I have to fix the Recall Device and go back. At least once."

"Why?"

"Because I have to leave the vest and your cross for Kyle," I answered.

"My cross? You mean this?" She pulled the cross from underneath her blouse.

"No, I mean this." I stopped and grabbed the envelope with the note and the cross from a pouch in my backpack.

"So there are two of them now?" she asked, frowning. "But don't I have to give this one to you sometime in order for that one to be this one? What if I don't?"

"Then you destroy the entire space-time continuum," I answered gravely.

"Seriously?"

"I have no idea." I shrugged. "By the way, I think you also have to, er, I mean, get to go back to the 1910s and be instrumental in the development of the Chronal Engine."

Emma put a hand up to stop Aki from attacking her hair. "You mean be a serving girl? In Texas? Before air conditioning? I don't think so."

We arrived back in the waiting room. A woman was there with a sick little girl, and they'd changed channels on the television so that it showed a purple dinosaur cavorting with a group of children.

We sat, trying to ignore the cheerful choruses. Emma set Aki down beside her, out of sight of the check-in booth.

"They make a cute couple, don't you think?" she asked, all of a sudden.

"What?"

"Kyle and Petra," she replied.

I grunted.

"Emma! Max!" The nurse spoke through the hole in her glass enclosure. "I just spoke with Mrs. Castillo. She says that Mr. Pierson is expected to recover."

We cheered and high-fived. And then were promptly hushed by the lady in the corner.

Emma looked puzzled. "Did we ever figure out why Grandpa knew about the heart attack beforehand?"

"I would guess," I said, "that at least one of us went back before

< 170 >

we arrived and told Grandpa about what was going to happen."
I hefted the resonant crystals in my hand. "It seems like a good
test jump, don't you think?"

"But what if it doesn't work?"

"Space-time continuum." I made an exploding motion with my
hand. "Poof."

As long as I can remember, two of the things that I've enjoyed reading most have been fiction and nonfiction survival stories and fiction and nonfiction about dinosaurs . . .

Literary Antecedents

Daniel Defoe published *Robinson Crusoe*, considered to be one of the earliest novels in the English language (if not *the* earliest), in 1719. Based in part on the true story of Scottish sailor Alexander Selkirk, *Robinson Crusoe* tells the story of the title character, who is shipwrecked on a tropical island for twenty-eight years.

Extremely popular, *Robinson Crusoe* spawned an entire genre of stories called "Robinsonades"—tales of lone individuals or small groups stranded in remote (undiscovered) settings without modern conveniences and who nevertheless are able to bring civilization and often technology to the savage wilderness.

It's no coincidence that the 1812 work about a shipwrecked clergyman and his family by Swiss author Johann Wyss would be called *Swiss Family Robinson*. (Both *Robinson Crusoe* and *Swiss Family Robinson* are referenced by various characters in *Chronal*

Engine, as they provide one link—among several—between Samuel, from the early twentieth century, and the rest of the group, from the early twenty-first century.)

Robinsonades remained popular throughout the nineteenth and twentieth centuries. One of Jules Verne's most popular works is the 1874 novel *The Mysterious Island*, the story of five prisoners of the Confederacy who escape in a hot air balloon that subsequently is blown off course to an island in the South Pacific that they name Lincoln Island.

Mid-twentieth-century Robinsonades include William Golding's *Lord of the Flies*, an allegorical novel published in 1954 about a group of English schoolchildren marooned by themselves on a Pacific island (which has been characterized as an anti-Robinsonade in that the children end up exhibiting brutish rather than civilized behavior); and *Gilligan's Island*, a television comedy from the 1960s about six eclectic people who are lost on a desert island after leaving Hawai'i on what was supposed to be a three-hour tour.

The 1960s also saw the publication of Scott O'Dell's Newbery Medal–winning *Island of the Blue Dolphins* (1960), which depicts a girl stranded alone on an island for eighteen years; the television series *Lost in Space*; and the comic book series *Space Family Robinson*—the last two relating to a family named Robinson who are stranded on planets in outer space.

Author's Note

Since the 1960s, a number of popular survival stories have been published for younger readers, including the Newbery Medal–winning *Julie of the Wolves* by Jean Craighead George (1972); the Newbery Honor book *Hatchet* by Gary Paulsen (1987); and *Far North*, by Will Hobbs (1996). Although not technically Robinsonades, as they relate to survival in the Arctic as opposed to being stranded on a tropical island, they have certain common themes.

Dinosaurs invaded the Robinsonade survival story realm not long after their discovery and popularization in the mid-nineteenth century. Sir Arthur Conan Doyle's novel *The Lost World* (1912) and Edgar Rice Burroughs's *The Land That Time Forgot* (1918) involve, among other things, intrepid explorers surviving in remote yet contemporary lands where dinosaurs still exist.

Michael Crichton's *Jurassic Park* and its sequel relate to modern humans being stranded on an island in the present day where genetically engineered dinosaur-like animals stalk them. While the whereabouts of the islands in the stories are generally known, these novels could be called Robinsonades (or perhaps even anti-Robinsonades) and almost certainly would be considered survival stories.

Chronal Engine as originally conceived was, essentially, a Robinsonade or survival story with a time-travel twist and a nod or two along the way to Jules Verne and H. G. Wells.

Author's Note

Paleobiology

I've always liked dinosaurs. One of the first books I remember owning was part of a nonfiction collection on dinosaurs that my parents gave me when I was in the first grade. Back then dinosaurs were regarded as big, dumb, slow-moving reptiles. What was called *Brontosaurus* was thought to live in swamps because it needed water to support its great bulk.

In the 1970s and 1980s, though, building on his own work as well as that of a handful of others, paleontologist Robert T. Bakker popularized the idea of warm-blooded, fast-moving dinosaurs. This image has been cemented in the public consciousness with the *Jurassic Park* books and movies, and the BBC television series *Walking with Dinosaurs*.

The science of dinosaur paleontology is changing every day. Almost weekly, new discoveries of dinosaurs and dinosaur behavior make the news.

This leaves a great deal of room in which a fiction writer can maneuver. At the same time, however, verisimilitude requires the development of a complete ecosystem and that attention be paid to the current scientific understanding of dinosaur behavior and appearance.

In writing *Chronal Engine*, I have tried to hew closely to what I could glean of this understanding. Where there is controversy, I have chosen what I hope is a view that is plausible and that also lends itself best to the story.

Author's Note

Chronal Engine is set in North America during the Late Cretaceous, between about sixty-five and seventy-five million years ago. During that period, dinosaurs were the dominant land animals. The weather was relatively hot and humid, and oxygen levels were slightly lower than today. The seas were higher. Owing to continental drift, South America was separated from North America; and Eurasia and North America were linked by land. The central portion of North America was covered by a shallow inland sea.

Much of the flora, though, would be recognizable to a modern visitor. The dominant plant forms were conifers—such as sequoias, redwoods, monkey puzzles, yews, and dawn redwoods—as well as ferns, cycads, and ginkgoes. Cypresses and cedars were also present. Flowering plants were developing, and trees such as dogwood, magnolia, birch, poplar, and sycamore were appearing. Rushes, lilies, and cattails had evolved, and ferns occupied many of the niches that would be occupied by grasses today.

Broadly speaking, the dinosaurs and other creatures specifically named in *Chronal Engine* reflect genera that were present in western North America in the Late Cretaceous. In particular, much of the fauna is based on the Late Cretaceous Javelina and Aguja Formations of Texas and the Ojo Alamo and Upper Kirtland Formations of New Mexico. Nevertheless, certain geographic and biostratigraphic liberties have been taken.

Mammals were generally small, rodent-like creatures and are

believed, for the most part, to have been nocturnal. Snakes and bees appeared during this era. Centipedes, scorpions, crayfish, turtles, frogs, spiders, and segmented worms were also present.

Sauropods, which were the dominant herbivores of the Jurassic, were largely extinct in North America by the Late Cretaceous, although they were present elsewhere, and fossils of the Late Cretaceous sauropod *Alamosaurus* have been found in the American Southwest. Recent finds suggest that *Alamosaurus* was one of the largest sauropods of all time.

The highly successful iguanodonts had largely been succeeded by hadrosaurs, such as *Lambeosaurus, Parasaurolophus, Corythosaurus, Anatotitan, Edmontosaurus,* and *Maiasaura.* The stegosaurs were extinct.

Tyrannosaurs—such as *Tyrannosaurus rex, Albertosaurus,* and *Daspletosaurus*—were the dominant land predators. As of this writing, there is controversy over whether *Nanotyrannus* is actually a separate species or simply a juvenile *Tyrannosaurus rex.* However, *Nanotyrannus*-sized tyrannosaurs (*Alioramus* and *Alectrosaurus*) are known from Late Cretaceous Asia, and a similarly small tyrannosaur (*Teratophoneus*) was recently discovered from Late Cretaceous Utah.

Smaller "raptors," or dromaeosaurs (like Aki), such as *Dromaeosaurus* and *Bambiraptor,* were also present, although the larger

Author's Note

genera, such as *Deinonychus* and *Utahraptor*, appear to have been extinct.

Other dinosaurs mentioned in *Chronal Engine* or extant in Late Cretaceous North America include *Troodon* (related to the dromaeosaurs), the armored ankylosaurs, the feathered oviraptorosaurs, the ostrich-like *Ornithomimus*, and the small alvarezsaur, *Albertonykus*. Horned dinosaurs like *Triceratops*, *Torosaurus*, and the smaller *Leptoceratops* were abundant.

Non-dinosaurian reptiles referenced include the crocodilian *Deinosuchus* and the azhdarchid pterosaur *Quetzalcoatlus*, both of which have been found in the Big Bend area of Texas.

Birds, which are believed to have descended from a dinosaur ancestor, were diversifying. Some still had teeth.

The dinosaur footprints at Max's grandfather's ranch are based on the many fossil track ways found throughout Texas and, particularly, on the famous tracks found in the 1930s in Glen Rose, Texas, now a part of Dinosaur Valley State Park. Other sections of these tracks may be seen at the American Museum of Natural History in New York City and at the Texas Memorial Museum in Austin.

I've located Max's grandfather's ranch in Bastrop County near McKinney Roughs Nature Park, although in reality that area is not known to be a source of Cretaceous dinosaur fossils or tracks. Like the ranch, St. Joseph's Hospital is fictional.

Author's Note

Many resources were consulted in the course of writing this novel, including several hundred journal papers reflecting current research (freely available online).

An excellent, thorough, and accessible reference is Thomas R. Holtz's *Dinosaurs: The Most Complete, Up-to-Date Encyclopedia for Dinosaur Lovers of All Ages* (2007). A-to-Z dinosaur encyclopedias are available from Dorling-Kindersley, National Geographic, Lorenz Books, and Firefly Press.

The Indiana University Press series Ancient Life was also invaluable and includes such titles as *Eggs, Nests, and Baby Dinosaurs: A Look at Dinosaur Reproduction* (1999); *Oceans of Kansas: A Natural History of the Western Interior Sea* (2005); *The Complete Dinosaur* (1997); *Tyrannosaurus Rex, the Tyrant King* (2008); and *King of the Crocodylians: The Paleobiology of Deinosuchus* (2002).

Gregory S. Paul et al.'s *The Scientific American Book of Dinosaurs: The Best Minds in Paleontology Create a Portrait of the Prehistoric Era* (2000), George Poinar et al.'s *What Bugged the Dinosaurs?: Insects, Disease and Death in the Cretaceous* (2008), and Louis L. Jacobs's *Lone Star Dinosaurs* (1995) also provided valuable insights into paleoecology.

Philip J. Currie et al.'s *Encyclopedia of Dinosaurs* (1997) and David B. Weishampel et al.'s *The Dinosauria*, 2nd ed. (2004), are comprehensive but probably of interest only to a professional paleontologist. Anthony J. Martin's *Introduction to the Study of*

Dinosaurs, 2nd ed. (2006), and Spencer G. Lucas's *Dinosaurs: The Textbook*, 5th ed. (2008) are useful introductory college texts.

Zofia Kielan-Jaworowska et al.'s *Mammals from the Age of Dinosaurs: Origins, Evolution, and Structure* (2004) and T. S. Kemp's *The Origin and Evolution of Mammals* (2005) provide sophisticated and graduate-level treatments of Cretaceous mammals.

Acknowledgments

This novel has been a long time in the making.

First, thanks to all the paleontologists who study and write and blog, and whose work and theories I was able to use to create the world of *Chronal Engine*. Any errors are, of course, my own.

I'd like to thank Anne Bustard for her questions on an early draft ("Does the gym teacher really need to be eaten?").

I also must thank my wife, Cynthia, for her support and willingness to visit every natural history museum in every city we've been to these last few years and her patience in watching paleo-related documentaries and pseudo-documentaries on TV and listening to me rant about them ("That would never happen!").

Finally, thanks to my agent, Ginger Knowlton, and my editor, Daniel Nayeri, for coming along on this jungle cruise to the Age of Reptiles.

GREG LEITICH SMITH lives in Austin, Texas, with his wife, author Cynthia Leitich Smith, and four cats. He is the author of *Ninjas, Piranhas, and Galileo* and its companion book, *Tofu and T. rex*. He and his wife coauthored the picture book *Santa Knows*, illustrated by Steve Bjorkman.

Greg has always been fascinated by dinosaurs and time travel. In addition to a degree in law from the University of Michigan, he holds degrees in electrical engineering from the University of Illinois and the University of Texas. Visit him at www.gregleitichsmith.com.

BOCA RATON PUBLIC LIBRARY, FLORIDA

3 3656 0603810 1

J
Smith, Greg Leitich.
The Chronal Engine

JAN   2013